POWER OF THE NINJA - FIRE

Silver Leaf Books Novels by T.J. Perkins

Shadow Legacy
Art of the Ninja - Earth
Power of the Ninja - Fire

Shadow Legacy
Power of the
Ninja - Fire

Book 2

By

T.J. Perkins

HOLLISTON, MASSACHUSETTS

POWER OF THE NINJA—FIRE
Copyright © 2013 by T.J. Perkins

Cover Art by Karim Whalen

First printing February 2013
10 9 8 7 6 5 4 3 2 1

ISBN # 1-60975-055-1
ISBN-13 # 978-1-60975-055-8
LCCN # 2012952996

Silver Leaf Books, LLC
P.O. Box 6460
Holliston, MA 01746
+1-888-823-6450

Visit our web site at www.SilverLeafBooks.com

CONTENTS

POWER OF THE NINJA - FIRE

"A ninja knows no fear – only targets."
Captain of the Black Dragon Squad.

PROLOGUE

Akira and I recoiled, pressing our backs against the wall. Fear gripped our hearts; we tried our best to keep our breath under control. The troll sniffed the air and lowered his head. A massive hand swiped at the darkness as it tried to find the strange odor that annoyed it so much. Finally, unable to take the frustration, the troll released a mighty roar, raised a spiked club high above his head and brought it down where we were hiding.

We sprang into action; unfortunately we went in opposite directions. The cuff chain pulled taut, jerked us to a halt and our feet flew out from under us. We landed on our backs and rolled to our sides. Akira and I were lucky the spiked club landed just in front of us. The troll must've seen our movement as we scrambled to our feet and backed up. It swiped a hand through the air again and grabbed the chain that connected us. He roared as he lifted us above his head and with all his might he threw us back to the floor. I landed on my side and felt a sharp pain in my ribs. Akira did a face plant on the floorboards, but quickly got up and looked at me. He had a bloody nose.

The troll bellowed again and reached for us. Answering bellows echoed along the walls as other trolls joined the hunt.

"We need to move as one," I shouted over the noise. "This way!"

With my weapon I slashed at the creature's lower leg and it rose up in pain. The other two trolls lumbered closer to see what the matter was and noticed our movements. They also became agitated and drew their clubs over their heads.

Akira and I stayed low to the ground. As our training took over, we moved together, avoiding the clubs that simultaneously smashed to the floor. We ran around the steps, weaving in and out of the troll's legs, and summarized that the troll's eyesight was bad, but their sense of smell was excellent. The creatures would pin-point us soon if we didn't do something.

We approached one of the subordinate trolls. Akira crouched low, on the balls of his feet, and gathered Ki to his legs. As soon as the creature turned to face him, Akira sprang up, slashed first at the creature's side, and then close to where the kidneys would be on the back. The troll shrieked as she slashed at him with long, dirty claws yet my movements on the ground distracted the creature enough for Akira to latch onto her long hair and swing to the ground.

The leader turned swiftly, swinging his club with so much force he took out the entire stair. Splintered wood flew in every direction and the troll roared in anger that he had missed us. Now on the ground, Akira tucked his kama into his sash, grabbed onto the cuff on his wrist and started to spin in a circle. I ran around him, faster and faster we went until I was airborne. My feet hit one section of the wall and I ran with my sword at the ready. I slashed at the leader five times before I flipped to land on the floor. The troll let out a blood-curdling howl.

The third troll decided to come to the rescue, but Akira had other ideas. He pulled out a few throwing stars and whipped them at the troll's lower legs. The creature screamed as they struck, one, two, three, up the side of his leg. Akira sprang into a dive roll and I moved with him. Side-by-side and completely in sync, we zigzagged back and forth until we were directly below the troll. I landed on one knee, the other positioned like a step, as Akira vaulted off my leg and slashed the troll across his neck with his kama.

Terrified of the tiny, horrible, biting things that hurt them, the trolls roared and turned to run. They slammed into the side of the building, smashed down a portion of the wall, and fell over each other. In their haste, they slipped on the wet rocks near the falls and fell in.

Akira and I stepped out into the fresh morning air and watched them.

I favored my side and watched the creatures thrash in the churning water. "I didn't think trolls liked the water."

"They don't," Akira said stifling a chuckle and wiped his bloody nose on his arm.

1

The Test

The nocturnal sounds of the forest filled the air as my team and I silently slipped through the brush. Our footsteps made no sound as we melted into the night, blending with the dark environment. Crouched low, our bodies tight, we moved as a unit, keeping an equal distance apart yet staying within sight of each other. Masakazu carried our weapon of choice, a bomb; our objective was to deliver it to our destination and blow up the building.

"You're doing well," Master Jun said in our headsets. "Remember your formation. Spread out now, but move as one once you get there."

"Got it," Shinji said.

"I'm all over it," Masa said.

I didn't respond. I was worried that Masa and Shinji would mess up the plan like they've done in the past. Not only that, I was more worried that if the strategy didn't go as planned I would lose my temper and seriously hurt someone again. Losing my temper was something I couldn't allow to happen; my career or life could actually depend on my restraint.

I had a history of temper tantrums - not the kind little kids have. Mine were violent; the kind that landed fellow Shinobi busted up, bloody and with broken bones in the hospital. All of my instructors, even Captain Yoshida, head of the Black Dragon Squad, had issued the warning to my uncle and made it quite clear that any more violent acts on my part would be dealt with in a most severe fashion. They never said what that meant, but I knew deep inside that it couldn't be good.

The stress of what was at stake played heavily on my mind and I took so many precautions that I wasn't focusing on the mission. I had lost my connection with the elements, distanced myself from the environment and didn't realize how disconnected I'd become until a twig snapped under my foot.

My team froze and crouched to the ground. Tension was heavy in the air. All eyes were on me.

"Duncan," Shinji whispered into our headsets.

"Duncan!" Master Jun growled in a low, commanding tone, "Concentrate!"

Shinji and Masa peered at me through the trees and brush. Though they were dressed in traditional black ninja garb and masks, concealed perfectly against the night and blending with the forest shadows, my trained eyes could still make them out. More importantly, I felt their presence. The worried looks in their eyes could not be mistaken from a fellow Shinobi and I immediately felt concern wash over me from both sides.

"Duncan, you okay?" Masa whispered.

It was a valid question. The guys knew I would normally never make such a stupid mistake. I released a deep breath and nodded, "I'm fine. We're almost there. Let's get this done."

Stealthy teamwork was only the beginning of a mission. The timing and response was essential. One slip up and a team member could get seriously hurt, or die. As team leader I couldn't let my personal issues compromise the mission.

We approached the outer wall. Guards were positioned all around the building.

"Shinji, Masa, go check the front and back entrances," I said. "Do not engage the enemy."

Without a word they disappeared into the night. Moments later their voices came over my headset.

"Four guards at the front," Shinji said.

"Two at the back," Masa said. "But only one on the roof."

Now that I knew the guards' positions we could move forward with our plan. "Regroup," I said.

Within moments we were at the southern wall, which was surrounded by forest. Gathering Ki in my legs I easily leaped into a very tall tree, caught the lowest branch and pulled myself up to the highest point. My target was the guard on the roof. He would spot us as soon as we approached the building. I had to take him out.

I removed a carved black bow from my back, laced it with an arrow and lined up. The bowstring strained against my grip until I let it fly. Though I could kill the man, that wasn't my objective. Ninja believed in preserving life above all else, rather than hastening the inevitable. Only when necessary did we kill. Keeping this in mind I made sure I had prepared my arrow accordingly. The tip had been dipped in a powerful and fast-acting sleep agent hours ago. The poison only needed to graze my target and he would go down, which was exactly what happened as the arrow nicked his lower leg just above his tabi boot.

"Area clear," Shinji reported after a brief moment of watching the roof. We wanted to make sure no one noticed the guard fall. "Looks like he was the only one up there."

"Seems a bit odd, don't you think?" Masa muttered.

I paused, raised an eyebrow and thought about his comment.

"He's got a point," Shinji said to me, nodding agreement.

It could be a trap, but time was running out. I could move forward and take a chance on being captured, or hesitate and not complete the mission. Either way – I failed.

"Well, Duncan?" Shinji prompted, "You're team leader on this mission. What do you want to do?"

I squinted my eyes in the dark, scanned the area, and watched the guards at the front of the building pace back and forth unaware of our presence. Yes, it could be a trap, and it was a risk, but all missions held an element of risk. It was all part of the thrill of special missions, night ops and training to become a Black Dragon.

"We go," I commanded quietly.

Without another word we laced our bows with arrows, secured with ropes and aimed them across the wide expanse of grass between the trees and the roof. The arrows lodged in the tarred roof with expert precision. We tied the other ends to the tree to create a single bridge and maneuvered to the roof using only our ankles and hands.

Our objective was simple: enter the building at the furthest point away from our goal, penetrate down to the bottom floor and plant the bomb in the center of the building. This building just happened to be the office of the Government Official, played by Akira, my long time rival. It seemed a bit ridiculous to enter the building so far away from our goal; however Master Jun wanted us to know what it would be like to do the mission when the situation wasn't ideal.

Shinji and Masa squatted down and crept to the side of the roof to watch the guards below, while I went to work removing the screws of an air vent. Once the vent opened, I dropped down to the floor below and gave a soft owl hoot to let my team know it was clear to follow.

The upper floor was pitch black.

"Night vision," I whispered to my team.

Our infrared goggles came in handy when it was too dark to see your hand in front of your face. The night vision lit up the hallway, turning everything red to our eyes, and made it easy to walk down a long staircase. Half way down we were interrupted.

"That's - far - enough!" came a loud commanding voice from the bottom of the stairs.

Busted.

The lights came on and we quickly removed our goggles. There were guards behind us at the top of the stairs and guards at the bottom. Accompanying them was the leader, Akira. At the moment it seemed we were trapped, but for a ninja the possibilities were endless.

"I know one of you has it," Akira said. "Hand it over."

Shinji looked at me and shrugged, Masa picked his teeth as if he didn't hear the question, and a slight smile passed over my lips as I stared intently at Akira. In a blur of motion I threw a smoke pellet in front of us. The explosion released a thick cloud that allowed the three of us to split up. Masa jumped the banister, and Shinji hid behind me, mirroring my body shape to make it look like he had disappeared.

"Don't let them get away!" Akira shouted. "Where's the third one? Go find him!"

The guards charged. Several of them jumped the banister and ran through the building in search of Masa. Shinji and I each grabbed a guard approaching from behind and threw them down the stairs into the oncoming group. They tumbled to the bottom steps in a heap, taking Akira with them.

"Damn it!" Akira shouted, getting up and pulling out his kama. "Give me that bomb!"

Shinji and I turned and ran up the steps; I went to the right, he went to the left. There weren't many places to hide, but that wasn't the idea. As soon as the guards hit the top landing we were on them. In a blur of fists and motion, Shinji and I sprang out of the dark and landed punches and back fist strikes until the guards were knocked back down the steps. Akira dodged their falling bodies and ran forward, kama drawn and ready to engage me. I drew my sword as I ran down the steps and met him head on. Sparks ignited as our blades clashed and we held each other's hard gaze, neither giving in yet straining against the other's strength.

"You lose, Duncan," Akira taunted, leaning in close to my face, "You and your loser team."

I felt anger well up inside me and a puff of air whipped my hair up off my shoulders. A knot of inner panic rolled in my stomach. I couldn't let the anger take over, not now, not like this. With my hatred of Akira I knew I would kill him if I didn't suppress it. Whatever this was, it had a mind of its own and if I allowed it the anger would take control of me. I would black out while my body reacted on its own. I wasn't going to allow that to happen again.

Just then Shinji slid past us down the banister, hit the floor running and headed toward our goal. It was the perfect distraction and even helped me reach a small element of calm.

"Stop him!" Akira shouted.

I used that opportunity to kick Akira in the chest, forcing him to stumble backwards, and then allowed myself to be captured by a group of guards that bumbled down the steps. It was a small price to pay for the good of the mission. The other guards ran off in the direction Masa and Shinji took.

"You still lose," Akira said, getting in my face and poking me in the chest with his finger.

"No, he doesn't!" came the commanding voice of Master Jun. Small yet powerfully built for a well seasoned retired ninja, Master Jun appeared out of the darkness and approached the bottom of the steps. He stood with his hands clasped behind his back and stared at us like a wolf sizing up prey.

"But sensei..." Akira started, and was silenced as soon as Master Jun put up his hand. Over the past few months Akira had learned the hard way not to argue with the Ops Training Sensei.

"Duncan and his team faced a difficult goal. To reach that goal he was willing to be captured so one of his team could plant the bomb and set it off. Masa accomplished this task. Your men were too late to stop him. Time was running out and Duncan had to make a crucial decision. Everyone in this building, including Duncan and his team, would've died once the bomb went off. Allowing himself to be captured was for the good of the mission."

"You mean..." Akira was slightly startled, looking from Master Jun to me.

"That's right," I shrugged off his guards, sheathed my sword and straightened my gi, "It was a suicide mission. That's what I chose. I took a gamble that we would come out alive, or at least one of us would, but was willing to make the ultimate sacrifice."

"That's stupid. Why would you do that?" Akira sneered.

"Because I wanted to know what kind of choices I would be willing to make in such a case. I wanted to know how far we would go when death was the most likely result."

I held Akira's glare, and then turned and walked down the stairs and into the night air.

Choices.

Uncle told me once that being a member of the Black Dragon Squad meant you had to come to terms with death. Every mission held an element of danger and the possibility of the ultimate sacrifice – by yourself or a fellow Shinobi. If captured you might even be tortured before you die, all while knowing no one was coming to save you. And I had sworn to him that when my time came I would face my choice without fear.

With the training exercise over I could relax. I had completed my mission, would be evaluated for my choices and would receive a critique of my performance. All of us had to go through this exercise as a team leader. Even though I hadn't seen him I knew Captain Yoshida had been watching, formulating in his mind who he would choose for the newest members of the Black Dragon Squad. If three retired from the squad, three were chosen – always a twelve-man squad, though no one understood why.

I sat on the front porch of the training building while students rushed around resetting the stage for the next test. Outside I sought solitude and enjoyed the sounds of the night, while I gathered my control. Unfortunately, loud verbal badgering rang out from Kenji, Makoto and Kikaku, as they rounded the building and spied me sitting alone. The distraction suddenly squashed my private time. These three were a group of older teens chosen for the pre-Black Dragon preliminaries. They'd already been through the training I'm going through now and for some weird reason I was the candidate they liked to pick on.

"What's the matter?" Kenji taunted, while the other two stood by his side and giggled quietly. "Akira too much for ya?"

I sat with feet shoulder width apart, forearms resting on my knees and looked at the ground. Though he was bigger and thicker than me, I could've easily sprung to my feet and beat the tar out of Kenji, but I didn't want to give him the satisfaction. Plus my girlfriend's best friend, Lilly would have a fit if I messed up his face. Besides, these three were also assistant instructors, I was to show respect to them. At the moment, they didn't shine like leaders in the least.

"Nawww, I think the mission was too much for him," Kikaku

said in a mocking tone. "Mayumi wouldn't want to be with a wimp."

The remark made my blood boil and I quickly turned my head and glared at him.

"Oooooo," they chorused.

"Better watch it. He just might kick your ass," Makoto said to Kikaku.

They laughed and walked away. My hard gaze followed their retreating forms.

Kenji and Makoto I could deal with, but Kikaku was a problem. He had the air of someone always up to something, sneaking around, plotting and planning some devious scheme. Exactly what that was, and more importantly, if he really *was* planning something, I couldn't be sure. At the moment all I knew was that he had eyes for my girlfriend, Mayumi. He was rude and in my face about it, not caring if I saw his approaches. And the more I thought about it the more I became convinced that his actions didn't make sense. Especially after I witnessed Kikaku having a private moment with a crazy kunoichi from the rival Shimoshuki Clan village.

Shi'tori had been her name, and several weeks ago she had made me her target. She wanted to know what it was my village kept secret and hidden – and she wanted my abilities. Neither of which I could give her. It was lucky, however, that she didn't know I had been given a Dragon Stone by a tengu. She probably would've wanted that, too. In a final desperate attempt at triumph she kidnapped Mayumi, led me on a dangerous motorcycle chase through on-coming traffic and hid in the forest high above the ocean cliffs. She was a deadly opponent, using tiny needles, darts and poisons. Unfortunately for her, my anger surfaced and took over, transforming me into...well...I wasn't sure, but she met her end in that forest. The reality of how I killed her still lingered in my mind, and the vision of her dead form ate at my conscience, but I got away with it and felt little remorse. It was survival, either she or me, and surviving is what I'd been trained to do. Dealing with her blood on my hands was hard to accept and I was still coping. I wonder how Kikaku would feel if he knew her body lay hidden and buried?

I recalled the moment when I stumbled upon Kikaku and Shi'tori's hiding spot behind the dojo, smooching and pawing all over each other. They acted as if they'd known each other for a very long time and had an established relationship. And I wondered how that could be when Shi'tori had only been in our village for two days. With Kikaku a pre-Black Dragon, he and the other guys were kept confined. That was Captain Yoshida's method, though no one understood it. So how was it Shi'tori and Kikaku knew each other so well? It was an answer I was determined to discover.

I recently had heard gossip from the other teens in class that Kikaku had started to disappear for hours at a time late at night. He took off alone and so far no one had been able to track him. If the Dragons knew I'm sure they'd drill him for answers. However, he wasn't officially a Dragon yet, so they probably weren't aware of the situation.

I was suspicious. If Kikaku had known Shi'tori, and she was from the Shimoshuki Clan, then perhaps that was the connection?

"Duncan!"

My thoughts were interrupted by the sharp tone of Master Jun. "I need you to play a guard this time."

I rose and followed him. Playing detective would have to wait, but when I found out the truth, what new choices would I have to face?

2

Walking the Path

As I sat on the front porch of my house the next day, my mind wandered and my head and heart still swam about all that had happened over the past few weeks: the tengu, the amulet, Mayumi and the kunoichi. I was still very much concerned about my anger issue and what had transpired when I was slowly dying of poison and under attack by Shi'tori. I was angry, out of control, and something was there inside of me – waiting. What made me 'transform' and kill her? What made me bury her body in a deep grave in the woods so no one would ever find her? Part of me understood that this anger saved my life and Mayumi's. That part I felt good about, but how to control it was another issue. I had to stay in control and be very careful to not flip out and beat the crap out of my fellow Shinobi anymore. If I did Captain Yoshida made it clear to my uncle that he would do 'what is necessary' – and that could be anything; arrest me, confine me or even kill me.

My recent conflict with Akira wasn't helping either and it just added to my stress level.

Reality started to set in. My friends and I weren't kids anymore; we were now young adults being groomed in the ways of the ninja arts to be the best assassins in the world, to fulfill a duty and uphold tradition. If we made the Black Dragon Squad our skills would be called upon at any given time, by any government – even our own – to carry out a mission of any kind, especially assassination. Until now, I hadn't thought of how serious life had become.

I thought, "*In two years I'll be done with training. I want to make the squad, but what if I don't? What will I do with my life? I'll need to get a place of my own. Where will I live? Should I marry Mayumi?*"

I leaned forward and rested my head in my hands; fear gripped my heart over these adult questions. It made my head hurt.

Just at that moment, my uncle and his friend Yamamoto strolled around the corner of the house, talking and laughing about days gone by.

"Yes, she actually said that," Yamamoto said with a wink. He leaned heavily on his walking stick.

"She must've loved you very much," Uncle Tou-Pang chortled.

"More like she loved my wallet," Yamamoto laughed as well and slapped Uncle Tou-Pang lightly on the shoulder.

They stopped joking around at the sight of me with my chin in my hands and looking depressed and cast each other an amused look.

"Ohhhh, good morning Duncan," Uncle Tou-Pang said in a loud, animated way.

I looked up, remembered my manners, stood and said, "Good morning Uncle, Yamamoto sensei." I bowed politely and stepped aside so the elders could walk past me.

My uncle slid open the front door, turned to his friend and said, "I'll make us some tea. Have a seat and I'll be right out."

"Oh, wonderful!" Yamamoto smiled, took a seat next to the Go table and propped his walking stick against the house. He cocked his head to the side and looked at me. "You don't seem very happy this morning, Duncan. Is something wrong?"

"Yes and no, sensei." I turned around, and sat on the wood porch again, leaning my back against the railing.

"Would you care to explain?" Yamamoto said.

"Well, I'm not sure where to begin. On the one hand I'm doing well in all my classes and I'm now in advanced weapons training, which is way cool. And on the other hand there are issues with some of the older guys, issues with Akira, of course, and now I have a special girl."

"You're always going to have issues with somebody, Duncan. Even at my age I have issues with some of the elders," Yamamoto said and rubbed his sore knee. "It's all about how you handle people."

I thought about this comment before saying, "I'm also worried I'll never make the squad."

"You have to get to the preliminaries first," Uncle Tou-Pang arrived with a tray of teacups and a warm pot.

I jumped up and took the tray from my uncle, waited for him to sit then poured tea for the three of us. I had a great deal of love and respect for the man and did all I could to help him. After all, when my parents died he raised me since I was a baby, and cared for me as if I were his own.

"Yes, that's right," Yamamoto took a cup and smelled the tea aroma. "There are The Trials for the preliminaries first. And you won't be prepared for them, I can tell you that."

"Why not?" I said.

"Because that's the whole point! They don't want you to be prepared," Uncle said excitedly. "They want to see how you perform under pressure, spur of the moment, caught completely off guard."

"You guys are worrying me," I said.

"Learn to master your fear. If you can be calm during a scary situation then you can respond perfectly. See? That's the key. To always keep your head and not let fear, or even anger, control the situation," Yamamoto said.

"Easier said than done," I said.

"You're right. Keeping it in mind is one thing, but to do it, is another. To keep calm in the face of danger, or during a disagreement, is the key. This helps you manipulate your opponent, think things through and come out the winner," Uncle said, pouring himself another cup of tea.

"So, staying calm, even when someone's making you mad, or when you're faced with a stronger opponent and you're scared, will help me think out the situation and beat that person?" I reasoned.

"Exactly!" Yamamoto laughed. "But remember, there are many different ways to beat an opponent, not just with your fists, but mentally." He tapped a finger to his temple and winked, "Psyche them out, you know?"

I liked the sound of that, and it reminded me of the mystical power of my Dragon Stone. So many stories and legends surrounded these amulets and stones and no one really knew the extent of their power. They could lend the possessor great knowledge, but could it also help psych out an enemy?

"Remember when I got this?" I pulled the red amulet out of my pouch. "Do you think this could help?"

Yamamoto sensei sucked in his breath; he obviously couldn't believe his eyes. Uncle stroked his short graying beard and peered closely. I felt triumphant as I held up the mystical jewel. It was neither a ruby nor a typical stone, and the jewel shone brilliant red as the sunlight reflected off its many faceted sides. It had the shape and cuts as if crafted from a master jeweler, neither square, nor round, but more oblong. It was encircled in a thin gold band decorated with tiny dragon scales, a gold clawed foot at the upper left and lower right to hold it in place, and a small loop so it could be worn by the possessor. Uncle Tou-Pang and Yamamoto did not reach out to touch the jewel, even though I offered it to them.

"I've heard tales about such things," Yamamoto said to my uncle.

"Indeed. The possessor will be given untold abilities," Uncle Tou-Pang nodded at the jewel.

"Like what?" I said. "I don't feel any different."

"Apparently the jewel will determine when it will reveal itself to you," Uncle Tou-Pang sat back and stroked his chin.

"Only one other person in our village has ever gotten one - Captain Yoshida," Yamamoto said.

"You mean the story where he was given the knowledge to defeat his enemy?" I stood and put the jewel back in my pouch.

"Yes. He told me that many years ago when he was in the heat of battle with a very strong foe, it seemed he was overwhelmed and going to die on this man's sword. A strange vision of his stone suddenly came to mind. Just at that moment, when he was badly wounded and it seemed all was lost, a strange feeling came over him and he found strength to stand and fight with the ferocity of a dragon. That's when he performed his famous Dragonfly move."

My eyes grew wide and I could almost picture Captain Yoshida doing the Dragonfly attack that I'd heard so much about all my life. Everyone knew the tale; how the Dragon Stone radiated an orange color and power flowed through him for a last desperate attack on his opponent.

"How did he know to do that particular move?" I said.

"You know, I asked him that same question and he didn't have an answer. He said it just came to him without thinking, like it was a natural thing to do," Yamamoto said.

"But, Duncan," Uncle interrupted, concern showing on his elderly face, "You can't relay on mystical items and your anger to help you in battle. You must unlock your inner animal fighting style, harness that energy to your sword, control it and call it forth at will. It's what will determine your place among the long line of assassins in our family and clan."

"I know that, Uncle." I was a bit snippy with my answer as I cast my eyes down, but not out of disrespect. Everyone my age or older got special, secret training to unlock our unique abilities. It's what was expected of us. My time hadn't come yet and I blamed it on the rage within me.

"Don't be disappointed in your lack of training, Duncan," Yamamoto said, placing a reassuring hand my shoulder. "You'll work through your difficulties."

"Sure." I didn't really believe it. "Of course I will." I forced a more positive look on my face even though I felt like a liar. "Well, I'm going to go find Hikaru now and hang out. Okay, Uncle?"

"Sure. Have fun and stay out of trouble," Uncle called as I bounded off the porch and headed into the village.

Hikaru's house was not far from my own and I took my time while cutting through busy Main Street, where all the vendors were. Here the town came alive with all kinds of shops, people selling clothes, household goods, fruits and vegetables, and almost anything you could want. Practically everyone knew me and waved and called as I passed. My favorite person was a shop owner named Ryu. He was a middle aged man with short neat hair and big build, his arms still had definition, his waist still showed where he used to be cut and ripped, and it was clear he must've been quite a warrior back in his day. I had never known him as a warrior, only as Ryu the cool shop owner that sold the best fruit in town.

"Hey Duncan," Ryu said wiping apples at a display. "How's it going?"

I walked up to the shop with its colorful banners, signs, and wind chimes jingling in the gentle breeze and looked at the crates of different fruit.

"I'm doing good, Ryu. And you?"

Ryu threw me an apple, something he always did, and said, "Oh, can't complain...that's on the house."

"Thanks!" I took a bite of the apple and noticed that someone was sitting close by.

Leaning against the shop and sitting on an empty crate was a slender and sickly looking boy named Morgan Shiratori. Smaller than most of the fifteen-year old boys, Morgan was quiet, lazy and kept to himself. He constantly had his face buried in a book and didn't have any friends. He was half American and half Japanese, pale skinned with light brown hair cut short in the back and long in the front, bangs sticking out crazy and hanging in his face. His whole appearance was what most American kids called Goth. Morgan topped it off with wearing three small gold hoop earrings in his left ear and reveling in wearing black all the time.

Orphaned at the age of nine, Morgan lost his parents in a car accident in Tokyo and was sent to our village to live with his aunt and uncle. Most people were under the impression Morgan had been traumatized by the loss and used that excuse to explain his oddness. Personally I didn't think Morgan was odd or strange at all. In fact, I felt Morgan liked being just the way he was and if people wanted to say he was traumatized that was fine by him, just as long as he was left alone. He didn't speak unless he had something important to say, he didn't hang out with others and, like me, he rarely smiled or laughed.

But I also knew that Morgan was very good at taijuitsu go-topo, The Art of Escape and inton jutsu, The Art of Conceal-ment and Camouflage, but hated weapons. He was also excellent with stealth skills and information gathering. This was discovered when Morgan was acing all his tests in every class for a month and it was revealed later that he had stolen the answer keys from the teachers then memorized each before destroying them. I smiled inside at the memory and felt I should acknowledge him.

"Hey Morgan," I finally said, thinking Morgan would only look up and wave, but not speak, like normal.

Morgan lowered the book he was reading and looked at me with a glassy-eyed expression. "Hey, what's up?"

I tried not to look too surprised that Morgan was actually en-gaging me in a conversation, and then looked at the title of the book he was reading; *1001 Gruesome Fates and their Out-comes, a Fantasy*. What in the world was he reading? I raised an eyebrow and shook off the creepy feeling before answering.

"Not much. I'm heading over to Hikaru's house. Wanna come?"

"Nah. I'd like to finish this." Morgan lowered his eyes back to the book and turned a page. "What was the outcome of you and Akira?"

I was a bit surprised that my latest confrontation with Akira at Night Ops Training already made the gossip head lines, but I played it off.

"Hum? Oh, that, nothing really. I got in trouble. My uncle wasn't real thrilled with me. I didn't think too many people knew about that."

"Are you kidding? It spread through the town like wildfire." He paused and turned a page before saying, "You know, I watch people a lot, listen to what's being said. Sometimes it pays to be an observer," Morgan said quietly and turned another page.

I made a mental note that he turned pages way too fast, but didn't acknowledge it. Instead I said, "What's that got to do with me?"

"I think that deep down Akira wants to be your friend...that he really does like you and just doesn't know how to go about getting along with you." Morgan looked up from his book and ran his fingers through his long bangs to adjust them in his face better.

"All he'd have to do is stop making rude comments to me all the time and eventually we'd start to get along." I crossed my arms, leaned against the shop and took another bite of my apple.

Morgan looked at me from over the book and said, "You know, sometimes you have to see things from the other person's eyes. There's drama going on with Akira, things you may not know about. It might be worth looking into." He shrugged and looked back at his book then said, "I'm just saying."

I stopped chewing and thought, *That's the same thing Yamamoto sensei said to me a while back. Well, not exactly, but its close enough. Maybe there's something in this idea after all?* After a brief pause I said out loud to Morgan, "Ummm, yeah, well...listen I'm heading out now, but if you change your mind you're welcome to hang out with us."

"That's okay, but thanks anyway," Morgan sighed, slouched on the crate even more and raised the book to hide his face.

"See ya, Ryu!" I called while waving.

I finished my apple and jogged off in the direction of Hikaru's house. On my way down the row of shops I passed a clothing store on my right. It was the main shop where everyone got their gi, pants, workout outfits and where Madam Yukia made all the uniforms for the Black Dragons. Not only that, but she had become a famous designer of martial arts uniforms for ninjitsu schools all over the world. Normally I wouldn't have hesitated, but shouting from inside the shop made me pause and listen. It was a father and son, they had their backs to me so I couldn't see who they were, but the voices sounded familiar.

"What's the matter with you?" the man shouted. "You constantly fight with that boy and tear up your clothes!"

"I'm sorry, okay?" the son protested.

"If you'd learn to fight properly, and not be wild with your strikes, maybe you wouldn't screw up all the time!"

"Nothing I do is good enough for you, is it?" the son shouted back.

A loud smack was heard; conversation stopped within the shop.

Embarrassed over what I'd witnessed, I quickly stepped away from the shop and continued down the street. A sick feeling lay in my stomach when I realized who the two people were - Akira and his father. Wow, that was a bit upsetting, even for me to witness. Maybe Yamamoto was right? Akira seems to be under a great deal of pressure to please his dad. Maybe Morgan was right? Seeing how others look at you, and how you look at others, could change the way you treat a person. I was lost in thought as I rounded a corner and approached Hikaru's house.

Mayumi was standing on the bottom step of his front porch, talking to Hikaru, and I paused at the sight of them. Hikaru was my best friend and I knew I could trust him with anything in the world, but not with Mayumi. Especially since I knew Hikaru had eyes for her and kept his distance only out of respect for me. But at the moment it seemed Hikaru forgot about that respect level. I wasn't sure why, but suddenly my heart started to pound and anger started to rise as a puff of wind blew up around my feet. Right now, as far as I was concerned, Hikaru was standing entirely too close, gazing into her eyes, making her blush and giggle and...oh, no he didn't!...he brushed her cheek with the back of his fingers.

Heat rose to my face and I clenched my fists as I moved forward with long, determined strides. I could feel my eyes becoming dark, thoughts of death and hatred filled my mind; my vision clouded slightly and the puff of wind around me churned into a strong breeze.

*Yes...*a whispering resounded in my head, faint and far away.

Pin pricks of dark visions flashed before my eyes. Death, destruction, and seeing Hikaru impaled on my sword tantalized my mind. A slight amused smile touched the corner of my mouth, but I slowed my pace, shook my head and regained myself. These thoughts were not my own and I wasn't sure why I would even think of such things. I stopped, took a deep breath and remembered Yamamoto's words, 'if you can remain calm even when someone is making you mad, you can defeat him.' I stared at the ground, unfocused the darkness building in my eyes and shook my head. What was I thinking? This was my best friend. I couldn't lash out at him like I'd done to others and especially not in front of Mayumi.

Stay...want to stay...

My mind cleared as I ignored the strange voice sensation, blowing it off as just my imagination in the heat of the moment, but the situation did not change and I suddenly felt calm enough that I could confront Hikaru without hurting him.

"Hikaru!" I called angrily as I once again steadily approached.

"Hey, dude, where ya been?" Hikaru waved and smiled.

Mayumi turned and smiled at me, warmth radiated off every inch of her as she took a step in my direction and threw her arms around my neck.

"Hey sweetie," she cooed and gave me a kiss on the cheek.

I wrapped my arms around her giving Mayumi a gentle squeeze then looked her in the eyes, our foreheads touched. The tips of our noses touched and she giggled. I looked over Mayumi's shoulder as I hugged her again. Hikaru's eyes meet mine and I flashed my best friend a very serious look.

"You staying?" I said to Mayumi.

"I've really got to help my mom clean the house. I was just talking and killing time. It wasn't a total waste though. At least I got to see you!" she said.

"You wanna hang out later? At my place? Maybe after dinner?" I said.

"Sure, but let me ask my mom if it's okay." She blew me a kiss, and then turned and walked away. My eyes followed her gently swaying hips until she rounded the corner.

The brief silence that followed was so thick you could slash it with a katana. Hikaru rubbed the back of his neck, placed a hand on his hip and cleared his throat several times.

"Um...wow...you and Mayumi, uh, you two are finally...ah, finally..."

"A couple...yeah..." I said sharply and averted my eyes to the ground.

"I-I didn't know...."

"Well, how could you know, I mean..."

"Yeah, like, when did this all happen?" Hikaru struggled to patch things up between us.

"A few days ago..."

"Really? Wow." He sighed.

"Yup."

"Hey, look...I'm sorry, dude, really. I was just, you know..."

"Yeah, I know," I said abruptly and quietly, now looking Hikaru in the eyes, calm filling my heart, yet still serious. It was a much better feeling than when I was angry just a moment ago.

But I think I finally got Hikaru to understand that he had stepped over that proverbial fine line and to not do it again. Even best friends have boundaries.

Hikaru blew out a heavy, nervous sigh, stepped closer to me and put out a hand, "Are we all right?"

Slowly one side of my mouth turned up in a half smile. I couldn't stay mad at him. I grabbed Hikaru's hand roughly and the two of us hit shoulders and slapped each other on the back in a brotherly hug. We started to laugh which released the tension that had built between us and I could tell, deep inside, Hikaru was afraid of me. The idea of such a thing really bothered me, but I decided that now was not the time to talk about it.

"We'll always be all right, Hikaru," I said.

"I see you brought your katana?" Hikaru said, wanting desperately to change the subject.

"All the time."

"For real. It's like another appendage," Hikaru laughed and pulled his from the sheath he wore on his hip, skillfully held in place by a red sash tied around his waist.

"Wanna work out? Class is tomorrow and we should practice," I said, reaching over my head, releasing the snap on the case and smoothly pulling out one katana.

"Hey, it didn't get stuck this time," Hikaru said, clearly impressed.

"So what do you want to do?" I said, taking up a stance while lightly flipping the sword handle around my hand like it was a tiny knife.

"Um, okay, let's do the three strike thing, back and forth. Then we can mix it up with adding a kick, just like we did in class," Hikaru suggested.

"You first," I motioned with my fingers for Hikaru to attack.

We went back and forth with the drill; Hikaru first delivered three strikes, while I blocked then I took a turn. After a few times at this I added in the sidekick, remembering the straw dummy I had destroyed in class and being careful not to kick my friend as hard as I actually could. I didn't understand this new strength brewing inside me and wasn't sure how to control it.

"Looking good, buddy," Hikaru said, showing off by taking on a low stance, leaning back on his left leg, the right extended almost straight out in front, with both arms open wide.

I shook my head and allowed a slight smile at his actions.

"Hey, you've been doing that a lot lately," Hikaru said.

"What?"

"Smiling. Well, sort of...it's not really a smile the way you do it. Now come on!"

I rushed forward, this time mixing up when I kicked during my strikes.

"I like it," Hikaru said with a short laugh, stepping in with his strikes.

At the third strike our swords clashed, hilts locked together, but I didn't retreat, I held my position, making Hikaru work for it. His strength matched mine and our faces twisted in the agony of a power struggle, muscles tense, toes of our tabi boots digging into the ground and neither wanting to give way.

"I ran into Morgan on the way here," I said, straining against my friend's power.

"Oh, yeah? He's creepy," Hikaru grunted, and pushed back.

We finally broke apart; our blades echoed a metallic *zing!* Hikaru advanced as we continued the conversation.

"He told me something about Akira that seems a bit strange," I said, countering Hikaru's kicks and strikes with a back flip, side roll then dashed to the nearest tree, ran up the trunk, executed a back flip over him, and landed directly behind him.

Hikaru spun and raised his blade, stopped my downward strike right above his head and said, "Anything coming from Morgan would be strange."

"He's not that bad. He's actually a handy guy to have around," I paused and backed away to catch my breath and put my hands on my knees. "He's an excellent spy, you know. Anyway, he mentioned that he hears and sees a lot from Akira; what's said, his life, how he really acts. He's under the impression that Akira actually wants to be my friend."

"No way!" Hikaru laughed, fell back into a stance and, without hesitation, delivered a front kick to my chest, knocking me to the ground. He continued his ground assault on me; repeatedly stabbing at the ground, slashing and sending up clippings of grass with each strike, and then followed up with a heel stomp.

I laughed and rolled this way and that, evading Hikaru's attacks like it was slow motion and child's play. Our blades clashed from time to time, but I tried using my feet and legs more than anything, trapping and blocking until I finally got a foot behind Hikaru's knee, kicked him in the chest, and sent him sprawling to the ground.

We lay still, breathing hard and sniggering at each other. I pulled up a handful of grass and playfully threw it at him.

"What in the world was that?" I finally said, quickly catching my breath.

"Oh, I don't know...I thought it would be cool to throw you off guard," Hikaru swiped at sweat on his forehead.

"Well, yeah, it was kind of cool," I muttered.

"I know, right?" After a brief pause Hikaru said, "Now, what's all this about Akira?"

"Oh, it's probably nothing, but Morgan seems to believe that Akira only hates me because of his personal problems."

"That doesn't make sense," Hikaru sat up and fixed the red ties at the ends of his long hair.

"I didn't think so either until I heard his dad yell at him in Madam Yukia's shop on my way over here. And get this, he was yelling at him for fighting with some boy and always tearing his clothes." I sat up and rested my forearms on my knees.

"You think he was talking about you?"

I shrugged, "Could be. I don't know of anyone else Akira fights with. And get this; his dad smacked the crap out of him right in the shop!"

"Ouch, that would hurt my pride more than anything else," Hikaru said, picking grass out of his shiny hair and combing his fingers through it.

"The other day Yamamoto sensei was talking about seeing how others view me. Like, seeing through someone's eyes, knowing their life, what's in their mind, how they think, blah, blah, and maybe I'd understand why someone feels the way they do about me," I rambled, trying to get my point across.

"Hmmm, that's pretty deep," Hikaru commented, now working on the other side of his hair.

"Cut that out, you're such a girl," I smirked and threw some more grass at him.

"Hey, the ladies like this," Hikaru said, springing to his feet and making sure the red ties at the ends of his long tails were secure. He picked up his sword and said, "Well, everyone knows Akira has had a real problem with you ever since you guys were nine years old." He sat on his front porch and grabbed his polishing kit. "First I hear he doesn't like you because you're mixed with Indian."

"Yeah, but that doesn't make sense. There are plenty of kids in our village mixed with something. Not like it's a big deal. It's just a little unusual that a woman from India hooks up with a Japanese, but still it's not a big deal."

"Then I hear he hates you because your uncle shows favoritism, which I think is a crock because Tou-Pang sensei is nice to all of his students. After all, he teaches the little kids," Hikaru said, rubbing the blade of his sword with polish and a soft cloth until it shone.

"I don't know. It might be worth looking into, you know? Find out what's going on behind the scenes. It shouldn't be too hard to listen and watch without being noticed."

"Or you could use a direct approach and take Akira out in the woods and beat him senseless, while interrogating him," Hikaru joked.

I thought about his option and entertained the idea for only a moment. "Not to get off subject, but have you heard anything more about Kikaku?"

"What about him? He's annoying."

"About him sneaking around late at night."

"It could all be rumors." Hikaru continued to rub his sword as he spoke. "Why does that guy bug you so much? I mean, I know you have issues with him because of Mayumi," he paused and looked me in the eye. "But seriously, what is it?"

"I just feel he has some connection to the attack on us weeks ago, and the kunoichi, and that all leads to the Shimoshuki. What if he's sneaking around for some underlying reason? Maybe he's a traitor?"

Hikaru studied me for a moment, tested my reasoning, and then resumed polishing his sword. We were silent. Nothing more was said on the topic and I decided that it was time to go.

"Well, thanks for the workout, but I better head home. Later!" And I bounded off the porch, my mind whirling with questions.

3

An Unusual Secret

"Listen up!" Master Katsumi shouted to all five members of our class. He paced briskly behind us as we separated and stood before thick wooden posts, a paper target attached to each. The morning was warm and mist from the forest curled across the ground and around our feet. Master Katsumi seemed very impressed with how well we were behaving today. "I want to see how well you've learned to throw kuni and shurikens. You've been doing this stuff since you were twelve, so it shouldn't be too hard. But we're going to do something a bit different. First, you'll reach into your pouches without looking, keeping your eye on your target, and pull out one of the two weapons I call out. You'll then throw it at your target. Understand?"

"Yes, sir!" we shouted.

I was ready. I crouched low with my right foot out, left foot back and left hand poised near my pouch.

Akira was next to me, taking on the same stance, looking at his target and not paying any attention to me. In fact, he hadn't said one word to me since class started. Perhaps it was best, I wasn't sure if I should to talk to him about what I had overheard yesterday.

"Shuriken!" Master Katsumi shouted.

All five of us reached into our pouches at the same time. Yuji was the first to produce a sharp pointed metal star and throw it at his target. Some of the others fumbled until they were able to find a star among their arsenal, but then quickly threw one and hit the target, but not a bulls-eye. I was one of those bumbling around and felt stupid.

"A little slow, people. This is not rocket science. If an enemy is quickly approaching you need to be able to stop him from a distance. That means you'll need to locate the appropriate weapon in your pouch and lodge it in the leg...or wherever... stopping him before he gets to you." He paused and looked at our class, making sure we were ready. "Now let's try that again! Shuriken!"

Along with the rest of the class, I quickly reached into my pouch again, this time locating a throwing star without hesitation and flung it at my target. Yuji was the only one that hit the bulls-eye.

"Much better. Very good, Yuji. Now back up." Master Katsumi waited until we walked backwards a few feet, "Now you're going to do a forward shoulder roll, come up into a crouch position and throw the weapon I call out. Understand?"

"Yes, sir!"

"Ready – shuriken!"

In unison, all five of us smoothly did a forward shoulder roll, barely touching the ground, so light and fast that not even a piece of dirt stuck to our gi. We came up into a crouch position; Yuji lost his balance, Mayumi leaned forward too far and threw her star into the trees, Hikaru, Akira and I were the only ones right on target.

"Come on, come on," Master Katsumi complained walking

in front of us. He stopped and put his meaty hands on his hips, looking us over with his good eye. His muscles rippled, and made the scars running down his arms dance like waves on an ocean.

I froze in place and watched the weapons master, afraid we would be punished with more pushups, especially since we were already on the ground. My eyes followed the tough and tenacious teacher as he paced back and forth in front of us.

"You can make this hard on yourselves, or easy," he said, starting with Yugi as he walked down his row of students. My eyes followed him as he paused to stare at each one of us in turn. "Because we're going to do this over, and over...and over." He glanced at Mayumi. "Until this becomes second nature, until you're so sick of it you could..." He now paused in front of Akira and looked at him before finally saying. "Puke."

Akira lowered his eyes to the ground at the mere mention of the word, obviously remembering our first day of class.

"Go collect your weapons and get back to the starting position! Move! Move! Move!"

We scrambled over to our targets, keeping low, knees bent and running full speed, stopped briefly only to grab our stars and dashed back to the start position.

"Roll and throw. Here we go! Kuni!"

The entire two-hour class continued on this way. We rolled forward once and threw a weapon. When we had gotten good at that Master Katsumi made us roll twice and throw a weapon. After about twenty minutes of that we had to run, dive roll and throw a weapon. Toward the end of class the weapons master finally had us shoulder roll, dive over a teammate, shoulder roll again, and then throw a weapon all at a dizzy-fast pace. By the time the two hours were up we were filthy. I was glad class was over; even I finally had to admit that my thigh muscles were sore from crouching down so much.

I sat on a small patch of grass near the weapons shack, gathering my books for Math and Biology, as well as my gym bag for taijutsu class. Mayumi walked over to me and bumped my foot with hers.

"Ready?" she said, leaning her face down to mine.

I couldn't help smile at her. Even with dirt smeared across her forehead she was beautiful. I reached up and playfully rubbed dirt from my finger on the end of her nose.

"Ewww, stop, I'm going to break out if I don't keep my face clean," she fussed.

"With pimples or without - you're still beautiful," I said softly, standing and slinging my bag over my shoulder.

"Tsk, disgusting," Akira muttered walking past us without a glance.

Yuji hurried to keep up with him.

Hikaru walked over to me and said, "At the risk of being the third wheel, you mind if I tag along to Math with you?"

"Sure," I flashed him a wry smile and draped my arm around Mayumi's shoulder. "We'll take Mayumi to her class first then go to Math."

I couldn't help but notice that Master Katsumi watched us leave, a look of concern showing on his face. Curious, I used my ninja skills to secretly watch him as he continued to watch us. His gaze followed us as a shadow came from behind him, but he didn't flinch or become alarmed. Instead I heard him calmly say, "Must you do that?"

"I could never fool you, could I?" Captain Yoshida said. His small yet powerfully built body appeared very tiny next to the towering Katsumi.

I slowed my pace and observed them from the corner of my eye. They continued to watch us as we rounded a bend and my curiosity piqued. Why were they watching us?

"Hey, guys, I forgot something back at the weapons shack. I'll catch up with you in a bit," I lied, while zipping off in the direction we had just come.

Once out of my friends' sight, I rounded a building and emerged behind the trees that bordered the weapons training area. I slipped behind the shack and eavesdropped on my senseis' conversation.

"It seems he has a mild distraction," Captain Yoshida was saying as he paced in and out of the weapons shack.

"Lucky for us it's putting his anger problem in check – for the moment," Master Katsumi said. The squeak of his chair told me he was sitting outside the doorway. "I thought he was going to kill Akira the first day of class."

"They remind me of you, me and Ami..."

"Don't go there, Yoshida, please," Master Katsumi interrupted him and released a heavy sigh.

"Sorry, but I see so much of the three of us in them. I'm afraid he'll lose her the same way you lost Ami, that's all," Captain Yoshida said before Master Katsumi could became angry or shout.

But Master Katsumi didn't shout, and as I listened I imagined he must have been remembering that fateful night. Uncle told me the story not too long ago when I started training more directly with the weapons master and became intrigued in his battle scars. He told of how an assassin from the rival Shimoshuki Clan was sent on a mission to kill Master Katsumi. Instead, the assassin took the life of the woman he loved dearly – Ami. He had never loved again since her death, and he proudly displayed the scars he endured from battling one of the toughest killers he ever encountered. It took six months to regain the use of his arms; he was permanently blind in his right eye. To him it was worth it to avenge the woman he loved -even though the killer got away.

I pressed my back against the weapons shack as they continued their conversation, especially since it was about me.

"Besides, this one is different," Master Katsumi said in a low tone.

Captain Yoshida snorted, "So you say. He's losing his heart to her and if something happens between them I'm just worried how he'll react. Will that anger get out of control?"

"We're all working with Duncan. Tou-Pang has done a great job with him."

"Is he ready for me?" Captain Yoshida demanded.

"You can't have him for another two years, Yoshida, you know that."

"The orange Dragon Stone tells me differently," Captain Yoshida persisted.

My heart skipped a beat at the sound of that and my curiosity grew.

Master Katsumi said, "You still got that thing?"

"Yep, sure do. And you know what?" he lowered his voice almost in a whisper. "It's awakened."

"What do you mean 'awakened'"?

"I've kept it beneath a floorboard in my home, locked away in a wooden box. Last week I was up early making tea when I suddenly heard a tapping sound. At first I couldn't figure out where it was coming from, but as I walked around my home I came upon an orange light coming from between the floorboards where I had hidden the Dragon Stone. The darn thing was glowing and jiggling around inside the box!"

"It's never done that before?"

"No. It's lain dormant ever since that last battle when I was young and it bestowed upon me the knowledge of the Dragonfly attack," Captain Yoshida said.

I sucked in my breath. Last week? That's when I got my Dragon Stone from the tengu.

"Why are you so worried? Maybe your stone is trying to tell

you that another battle is coming and you'll need it again?" Master Katsumi said. I could hear him lean back on the legs of his chair and prop his feet up on a nearby barrel filled with staffs.

"I can't figure it out, but every time I touch it I get a vision of a red Dragon Stone. Something tells me that someone special has acquired a stone recently," Captain Yoshida said, with a hint of mischief in his voice.

"What's this got to do with Duncan?"

"Many who were involved with his parents know of the gift his Indian mother, Anju, bestowed upon him. She was a spy just like his father, Kaito. She was spiritually in charge of 'It' and had to keep the 'Thing' safe; especially from that power-hungry man from Germany. You know the story, Katsumi. Duncan carries something very special inside of him, something only people from India truly understand."

Gift? Thing? It? What in the world are they talking about? Was the voice and my powers actually an It? I thought, but kept still to hear more.

"The Japanese are not so ignorant, Yoshida, don't sell us short," Katsumi snapped.

"That's not what I'm saying, old friend. It's just that we don't fully understand their culture and beliefs, and if we did maybe it would explain exactly what it is that resides in Duncan, why we must fear his anger and why my stone has been projecting images of his face among its facets," Captain Yoshida said.

I heard Master Katsumi put his feet down and shuffle in his chair.

"So he's the other person with a stone, huh?"

"Either that or my stone is issuing a warning about him. Danger, perhaps. Not much is known about the Dragon Stones. Only the tengu know their true power. Duncan *is* the one with the red stone, and if he has it and gains understanding of his abilities..."

Here we go again. Abilities, I thought, *If they only knew that I've already tapped into enhanced hearing and eyesight and embraced a power that I couldn't yet understand they'd probably lock me away.*

"He can't get angry, that's for sure. He could go either way – good or evil," Master Katsumi said.

"I've already issued the warning to Tou-Pang about Duncan's actions against fellow Shinobi. I don't want to do it Katsumi, but if he continues to lose control he'll leave us no choice. He needs to fully understand compassion, to master his anger, stay calm and focused. If he can harness these primal human traits it could help. That's why I want you to train him separately."

"What? You know I can't do that," Master Katsumi must've stood so fast the chair clattered to the ground.

Wow, personal training from the Master, I thought and my stomach did flip-flops in anticipation.

"Please, Katsumi. I want him as early as possible, perhaps sometime this summer. I know he'll be the youngest to ever make the squad, but I feel that I can guide him through these rough teen years. He's vulnerable right now, his emotions are unstable as with all teens, and if allowed to sway one way or the other..."

"Yeah, yeah, I hear you." I heard Master Katsumi interrupt him and blew out a nervous breath. "Look, why don't you let me talk it over with Tou-Pang. Let's see what he says. After all, it's his nephew."

"I appreciate it," Captain Yoshida said, stepping out of the weapons shack. I heard the crunch of his tabi boots on the gravel, a signal that he left.

With the conversation over I melted into the trees and shadows and hurried to catch up with Hikaru. I couldn't be late for class.

4

Ghost Stories

I wiped the trickle of blood away from the corner of my mouth with the back of my hand. Taijutsu class started off not so good. Once again, I had to pair up and work drills with Makoto.

"Oops." Makoto smirked, resumed a fighting stance and looked almost playfully at me from around his raised gloved fists. Even though he had gloves on, they weren't the typical extra padded gloves used in boxing; these were thin, almost like weightlifting gloves. Standard issue, black, and everyone had a pair. They allowed the wearer to clench their fists and feel contact with their partner.

I was tired of feeling contact from Makoto's fist to my face, and it irritated me that Makoto would smirk every time he got a shot in through my defenses. I was also getting angry at myself for allowing it to happen, and Makoto's cocky attitude wasn't helping. I felt a burning in my stomach, my heart began to race and I started to get mad.

"You're supposed to be careful with your teammate, jerk," I

quietly spat. "You can wail on the heavy bags."

"Come on, tough guy. Let's see what'cha got," Makoto replied softly with a flippant attitude, feeling entirely too confident.

I took a deep breath and tried to calm down so I could think straight. The commanding voice of Suzuki sensei made everyone stop the current exercise and turn to face him.

"All right everyone. Now we're going to do something a little different." He positioned himself in the center of the dojo and motioned for a student close to him to step forward to be used for demonstration. "Okay, your partner will grab you by your gi. The first thing I want you to do is sink; bend those knees. Using your partner's momentum, step behind his leg, getting in close, then take the palm of your hand, push up on his chin and...." He demonstrated the technique on the student so quickly and gently that the young man was on the floor without making a sound before he had a chance to blink. "Everyone got it? Okay, let's go."

Makoto and I squared off.

"It's my turn to attack," I reminded him.

"Yeah, yeah, whatever. Just go," Makoto grumbled and rolled his eyes.

Still fuming over Makoto's earlier punches, I grabbed his gi with both hands, held tight, and waited for him to perform the takedown, which he did flawlessly, ending with slamming me on the mat a little too hard.

I did a backhand spring to my feet and suddenly turned on Makoto, grabbed him by the throat and squeezed as a puff of air blew my hair off my shoulders.

"That was uncalled for," I growled low and sinister. I could feel my eyes cloud. The look from Makoto told me that he saw something odd in my face. I wasn't sure what and I didn't care, I just squeezed harder as he tried to break free.

Makoto grabbed me by the wrist and proceeded to perform a grabbing technique, which should've put me into an arm-bar and off his throat, but his idea fell apart instantly. Instead, I countered with a twist of my body and spun around to immediately get behind him. I then latched onto Makoto's gi, turned him around and yanked him close; nose-to-nose. I instantly stepped behind Makoto's leg, placed the palm of my hand under his chin and, instead of just putting him gently on the ground, I spread my whole hand over Makoto's face, literally controlling him this way. The entire move took only a few seconds and was done with so much force that I lifted Makoto off his feet and into the air, looking briefly like he was lying on an invisible bed. At that point, I took him down. I landed on one knee and slammed Makoto to the mat, flat on his back, with so much force and such a loud slap it made everyone in class stop and stare.

Makoto just lay there, moaning, and blinked his eyes open.

"Don't be rough with me anymore. Got it?" I sneered quietly and loomed in close to Makoto's face.

"Duncan!" Suzuki sensei shouted from the other side of the dojo.

I quickly grabbed Makoto by the wrist and hauled him to his feet. "Play along, you got me?" I growled quietly in his ear.

"You all right, Makoto?" Suzuki said.

"Yes, sensei," Makoto said, still a bit dazed and confused.

"What's gotten into you?" Our sensei looked at me strangely.

I respectfully bowed to him, "Nothing sensei. I guess I got a little carried away with the exercise."

I wasn't about to get in trouble over this. Makoto had it coming. For a very long time I'd been his punching bag, dealing with his foul play. But I had a gift, a power inside me somehow; Master Katsumi and Captain Yoshida knew about it, my uncle, too. It had something to do with my anger and right now I was having a difficult time controlling it. In fact, I was enjoying it.

Suzuki sensei looked at us, not quite sure what to say or do. Makoto looked all right and I did my best to sound truthful enough. After a moment he finally said, "Hit the showers. Everyone! Hit the showers!" He turned on his heel and walked away, heading for his office.

Class was abruptly dismissed and I thought this was a very odd thing for sensei to do. I let go of Makoto and sniggered when he fell to the mat on one knee. He hadn't quite recovered. I felt vindicated, even a little mean, and it radiated strength through my body – I liked it. A part of me wanted to stop, knew it was wrong, but I couldn't because there was another part of me that wanted to keep going.

"What's the matter, buddy? You can dish it out, but can't take it?" I stood close and looked down on him.

"I never tried to hurt you. What you did just now was no ordinary move." Makoto finally stood on shaking legs as he staggered toward the locker room. "What'd you do to me?"

"I hold back a lot. I'm a lot stronger than you know...than any of you know. A lot of you guys pick on me because you must think I'm a pushover. Well, I'm not. I'm more on your physical level, if not beyond, than you think."

I turned to walk away, but stopped at the sound of Makoto's voice.

"Oh, we've all heard of the things you can do. You run up trees, bound off rock walls, trees, or anything, and look like a blur while doing it. You can do flips; almost suspend yourself upside down in the air while attacking a target. Oh, yeah, everyone knows," Makoto hobbled across the mat and struggled to keep up with me.

"Is that why you guys pick on me?" I slowed down, but didn't stop.

"I...well...I don't know. It's just...it's just that all the adults talk about you like you're something special. A lot of us hear things, you know, like you're a little prince in disguise and it's some big secret. Nobody likes that, it's like special treatment and we've all been raised that the instructors don't have favorites in their classes. We're all equal."

I stopped and rounded on him. "You think I asked for that treatment? I have no idea what's going on, or why, or what's in the adults' heads! I wish somebody would tell me!" I headed for the locker room.

"Kenji and Kikaku have figured out that it has something to do with your mom and dad...and possibly your sister. The elders aren't happy that she took off. They're all under suspicion she's become a high-classed thief."

"Shut your mouth!" I turned and closed in on Makoto again, grabbing him by his gi.

Makoto flinched and stared at my eyes.

"What's up with your eyes, dude?"

"What?" I let go of him and turned away. I had to relax and stop letting the anger control me. Like Yamamoto sensei said, stay calm even in a tense situation and you can think you're way out of it. As I reached for the calm in my heart the nastiness that had taken over quickly dissipated. It was sudden, abrupt and the change scared me, but I wasn't about to show my fear to anyone.

Makoto pointed. "Now it's gone. J-just a s-second ago your eyes instantly became dark, like the entire eye, the white was totally gone. They were like black stones," He tried his best to explain, but acted entirely too freaked out.

"You're crazy," I muttered, waved him off and headed into the locker room. I knew I could feel a cloudy film cover my eyes when I got angry, but I had no idea that the entire eye was physically changing in the process. Why hadn't somebody told me before? I wanted to ignore Makoto and get away from him. My pace quickened.

But Makoto pursued me saying, "No, Duncan...h-hey Duncan, seriously man. That was freaky, like possession or something."

I entered the locker room with Makoto following. Kenji and Kikaku were gathering their gear, but took interest as we entered.

"Who's possessed?" Kenji chimed in with a laugh and acting like the big man on campus, while pulling items from his locker.

"No one." I said and flashed Makoto a warning glance, but was quickly cut off by Kikaku.

"Wooooo, I'm a scary ghost trying to possess you...ha, ha," Kikaku teased, wiggling his fingers in front of his face.

"Whatever," I grabbed my bag out of my locker, slipped on my tabi boots and walked toward the back entrance.

The three quickly grabbed their bags and followed me outside. They found an opportunity to torment me again and weren't going to leave me alone. I had to get away from them so I could calm down. Fortunately Mayumi, Shinji and Masakazu were waiting for me outside the door.

"So, what, are you possessed or something?" Kenji persisted with his questions.

"What are you guys talking about?" Mayumi stepped between Kenji and me and stopped the pursuit with a hard stare.

"Oh, scary stories. I love scary stories," Masa said excitedly, anxious to be part of the conversation. "Especially when they're based on reality."

I was grateful for the interruption.

"I think the scariest story is about the old watermill on the other side of the waterfall," Shinji said, keeping the topic interesting.

"Oh, I've heard that one," Kenji said, taking over the conversation and forgetting about his question on possession. "This old homeless man was wandering the countryside, looking for work, but he didn't tell anyone he was homeless - he was too embarrassed. The owner of the mill gave him a job. The old man would leave when the workday was over, but came back after it got dark. He snuck in and slept on the fourth level."

"What's so scary about that?" I said, not all that interested.

"Apparently, the mill would run all day and night because of the water flow turning the wheel constantly. Not wanting to be seen sneaking in, the old man would climb the spiral steps that encircled the wheel gears without the use of a lantern." As always Kenji paused for effect and was thoroughly enjoying the attention with everyone hanging on to his every word. "One night, he slipped and fell...down through the shaft...into the thick wooden gears. He was instantly ground up."

"Ewww," Mayumi said.

"His body was found the next day, mangled and twisted four stories below in the shaft," Kikaku said. "The workers found his lantern and matches next to his bedroll on the fourth level. He should've used that lantern when he walked up the steps."

"Almost every night you can see a light floating around inside the mill, like someone's walking around with a lantern," Kenji finished. "It's like his ghost is trying to correct his mistake."

"Nobody goes up there anymore," Masa said.

"Yeah, I've heard the elders say the trolls, you know, the mountain spirits, have taken over and will attack anyone going up there," Shinji added.

"I've heard that too," Mayumi said.

"What a crock," Kenji scoffed. "Those stories are told just to keep little kids from wandering off and exploring."

"A trip to the old mill is part of the Black Dragon preliminaries. We have to go up alone and spend the night," Makoto said.

"Have you done it yet?" I said, looking at Makoto with a silent challenge and for some reason I found his statement hard to believe.

"Well...no...the three of us haven't been assigned that task yet," Makoto said. "But the guys currently in the Black Dragons told us all about it."

"And you believed them?" Shinji said with a laugh.

"They're just yanking your chain," Mayumi said with a smile.

"Probably setting you up to see if you'll go check the place out," I crossed my arms and shook my head at the thought of my three rivals being made to look like fools to the squad members.

Trying to turn things around Kenji said, "Bet you wouldn't go up there." He gave me a hard stare.

"Oh, yeah, well I took you up on your last offer and beat a tengu! I can do this one too!"

"You what?" Makoto shouted in disbelief.

"That's right," Mayumi said, "I was with him. The tengu attacked me too, but we chased it away."

"So you think you have a lot of guts, huh?" Kenji crossed his arms and leaned in close to my face. "All right, tough guy, go ahead. I dare you to go up to the old mill and spend the night, just one night - alone."

"You're on!" I said. "I'll do it tonight!"

Just at that moment Akira walked quickly around the building with his little cousin, Haru, following close on his heels.

"Just show me how to work them, Akira, please!" Haru pleaded, jangling a pair of long-chained silver handcuffs at Akira.

"I already told you, I don't think you should be playing with them," Akira grumbled.

Akira was so busy fussing at his little cousin that he didn't realize he was walking into a crowd of people until it was too late and he plowed right into me.

"Why don't you watch where you're going?" Akira snapped

at me, not wanting to admit he was wrong.

"You've got a lot of nerve," I said, raising my fist.

Mayumi grabbed my wrist to keep from punching Akira. "Oh, no you don't!"

"Akira, please work these!" Haru whined and pushed between Akira and me regardless of the danger of getting hurt in a scuffle. He held the handcuffs up and jiggled them right in our faces.

I snatched the handcuffs away from the little boy.

"Why don't you just answer the kid and help him?" I looked at the handcuffs and tried to get them to close. "Sorry kid, it looks like they're broken. See? They won't stay closed."

"Give me those!" Akira snatched the cuffs away from me, "You just don't know how to work them."

"Do so! Give them back!"

"Oh, Mr. Perfect knows everything!"

"Shut up! Just let go, I can work these!"

What happened next threw me into shock. Kikaku reached out and in a blur of hand motion wrapped the open cuffs around our wrists. I guess he couldn't take the immature squawking anymore. There was a gut-wrenching *Click! Click!* which made all the arguing stop instantly. Akira and I just stared at the handcuffs, securely fastened around our wrists, eyes bugged and mouths hanging open.

"What'd you do?" I turned furious eyes on Kikaku.

Kikaku allowed one corner of his mouth to turn up in a wicked half smile then looked around me at Mayumi and gave her a wink.

"You idiot! Get these off!" Akira turned to his little cousin and said, "Here, give me the key."

"I don't know where it is," Haru whined.

"Well, go home and find it – quick! I can't stay like this!"

Haru ran off, half in a panic and half crying.

"Ha, ha! Good luck with your trip to the old mill tonight, Duncan," Kenji sneered, as he walked away.

"If you need company tonight, Mayumi, just give me a call," Kikaku said with a wink.

Kenji, Makoto and Kikaku strolled away and left us in shock about Akira and I handcuffed together. No one was sure what to do about it.

"I don't believe this," I sighed.

"What trip to the old mill?" Akira said, trying to squeeze his wrist out of the cuff. As he pulled and jerked the cuff cut into me.

"Ow! Stop it!" I shouted, "Kenji dared me to go spend the night at the old watermill and I took him up on it."

"Oh, what, are you afraid?" Akira taunted.

"No! It's supposed to be a preliminary trial you go through for the Black Dragons and, once again, Kenji thinks I can't do what they do. So, he dared me. I'm supposed to go alone. Tonight! I can't do that now!" I tried to squeeze my hand out of my cuff as well.

"Cut it out, that hurts!" Akira complained.

"Dude, this is messed up," Masa said, hands on his hips.

"How are you supposed to go tonight?" Mayumi said, "For one thing, your uncle is not going to allow it. And even if you weren't handcuffed to Akira you're to do this alone. How are you going to pull this one off?"

I thought about the situation for a moment. My friends were silent. We watched as Akira frantically struggled to get his hand out of the cuff. I wasn't real thrilled with being cuffed to him for any length of time either.

"I guess I'll have to lie to him. I've never done that before."

"You mean to tell me you've never, ever lied to your uncle?"

Akira stopped struggling and stared at me.

"No, I haven't. I have too much respect for him than to do that. If you're finding that hard to believe then you must lie to your dad all the time!"

Forgetting that we were attached, Akira suddenly pushed me, throwing me off balance and forcing me to fall to the ground. I landed on my back with a *whumph!* The long chain of the cuffs pulled taut, jerked Akira forward, and forced him to fall on top of me.

"Get off me!" I shouted.

With a bit of difficulty we struggled to stand.

"Okay, the first thing you need to do is find a way to get those off," Shinji said, "You still have at least five hours of daylight left to figure something out."

"Right. Let's go to my cousin's house and see if he found that key," Akira jerked the cuff chain and forced me to follow him.

"I'll take your stuff to my house, Duncan," Mayumi called after me.

"I don't know how they're going to pull this one off," Shinji said to Mayumi and Masa as we turned to walk away. He shook his head and handed Mayumi my books and bag. I heard him say, "And you know that Duncan's going up to the mill tonight, no matter what he has to do, just to prove something to Kenji."

He was right. My determination was piqued, but exactly what was I trying to prove? Whatever it was, it would be resolved tonight if I could make it to the old mill and face all of its haunting qualities.

5

The Old Mill

I reluctantly followed Akira to his little cousin's house and patiently allowed him to lead me around like a dog on a leash, while he helped Haru look for the tiny key.

"It's gotta be around here somewhere, Haru," Akira fussed. Dresser drawers slammed and books and papers tossed all over the room in search of the key.

"It was on my bed this morning." He dumped a container of action figures on the floor making an abundance of clatter.

"What's all the noise about?" Akira's Uncle Genkichi appeared in the bedroom doorway. He looked at us and concern showed on his face. Akira groaned, drooped his head and held up his wrist to reveal that we were cuffed together.

"Ohhhh, I see," his uncle said, trying not to laugh. "I thought I told you not to mess with those things?" he said to Haru.

"It wasn't his fault. One of the older boys in my class grabbed them and did this," I explained. "He thought it was a funny joke."

"Its no laughing matter," Akira cast an annoyed look at me.

"Did you find the key?" Uncle Genkichi said.

Haru shook his head, "Not yet."

"Keep looking," Akira demanded.

Frustrated, we went outside.

Once out of earshot I wheeled around and pointed a determined finger at Akira; "I'm going to the mill tonight no matter what, so we better go to your house so you can get some stuff."

"Ahhh! I can't take this," Akira whipped out one of his kama and started using the pointed end to pry apart the long chain holding the cuffs together. He twisted and jerked at the chain like a madman, causing the cuffs to dig into our wrists.

"All right, all right! Stop!" I yelled, "Face it; we're stuck together for the night. Let's just go to your house."

We didn't speak on the way to Akira's house, each lost in our own thoughts of how we were going to hide the fact we were handcuffed together and also to get out of the house for the night. A solution presented itself as we crossed the lawn and Akira noticed his dad had hung their clothes out to dry. He snatched one of his T-shirts off the line and draped it over our hands, hiding the cuffs and chain, and then casually strolled into the house.

His father was sitting at the kitchen table reading the local newspaper. At the sound of footsteps he looked up and was quite surprised to see the two of us together. It was all I could do to not think about the day I passed by Madam Yukia's shop.

"Hi dad."

"Good afternoon, sir," I said with a respectful bow.

"What's going on?" Akira's father said, narrowing his eyes suspiciously. He struck me as a hard man, not very loving or close to his family. Hard work and getting right to the point seemed to be his philosophy.

"Well, you see, Duncan and I have been talking and....you

know...we'd like to hang out together tonight," Akira struggled to get his thought out, and I could feel him get nervous under his father's hard gaze.

"I suggested he spend the night at my house...do guy stuff... and get to know each other better," I added.

Akira's dad stared at us for a moment then flicked the newspaper and said, "Good idea. I'll see you tomorrow after classes."

"Yes, sir," Akira said, leading me down the hall to his room.

Akira's bedroom was a modest size, he had a small bed, a large dresser and a closet full of gi tops, pants, tabi boots on one side, and jeans, shirts and tennis shoes on the other. Perfect for a young ninja and clearly showing his separate lives. Posters of rock bands splashed the walls and a bookshelf was filled with high fantasy novels, schoolbooks and CDs.

"Is your dad always so cold?" I said.

"Shut up!" Akira was in my face fast.

I thought it best not to respond, just in case his dad would hear us through the walls. Instead I gazed at all the things in Akira's room.

"Wow, you like the same bands I do. And you read the same books, too," I said.

"So what? You're not on a grand tour, you know," Akira grabbed a few personal items and stuffed them in a small bag then flung it over his shoulder. "Let's go."

Twenty minutes later we arrived at my house and tried the same lie on Uncle Tou-Pang.

"And I'd like to hang out more...doing guy stuff...over Akira's house," I tried to be as sincere as possible.

"Well, I don't know," Uncle Tou-Pang said, stroking his beard.

"Remember what you and Yamamoto sensei told me?"

He was silent for a moment, reflecting back on the conversation the three of us had just the other day.

"Well, I guess it will be all right. But you have to be up and to class on time, Duncan."

"Yes, Uncle," I bowed respectfully and led Akira to my bedroom. My stomach hurt and I knew it was because I just successfully lied to my uncle for the very first time; I had deceived him – and he trusted me.

My room was quite large, a dresser, bed and closet much like Akira's, but with a desk against one wall, area rugs on the floor, various plants scattered around the room and a tabletop waterfall was on my bedside table. I also had rock band posters on my wall, but had more of a display of swords and weapons from all over the world that my uncle had collected and brought as gifts over the years. Akira snorted at the display. I ignored him and felt the one-hour walk up to the old mill would be a good time to hash things out. Just like Hikaru said, take him out in the woods and...well, talking would be better than beating him senseless. Before I walked out, I grabbed my swords and slung them on my back.

"Let's go," I said to Akira.

We walked in silence for the first thirty minutes, cutting through the trees and roughly pulling each other around boulders and natural barriers. We each tried to take the lead; neither allowed the other to choose which direction to go. The anger between us was rising and it didn't help when we came to a split in the path. I turned to the right, while Akira turned to the left. The two-foot long chain pulled taut and the cuffs cut into our wrists, jerking us to a stop.

"What are you doing? It's this way," I snapped.

"It doesn't matter which way you go, the paths join further up the hill," Akira said, jerking the cuffs and forcing me to take a step in his direction.

I planted my feet and gathered strength and said, "No, it doesn't. This is a direct path. That's the long way." I then jerked the cuff with so much force it threw Akira off balance and drew him over toward my path.

"You really don't have a clue, do you?" Akira jerked the chain in his direction.

"You mean, you don't." I yanked him in my direction.

"Stop it!" Akira jerked back.

"You stop it!" I fought him until we were face to face, holding our cuffed hands up in a fist like we would punch each other any minute.

The tension was thick, electricity from our inner Ki radiated off of us, sparking at points in the air around us. It's what made us what we were, or could destroy us if we didn't properly harness our inner energies. We held each other's gaze, both unrelenting, both stubborn and set upon our path. And as we stared into each other's eyes I came to the realization that the battle would never be won, and the arguing would never stop until one of us became the bigger man and took a step back.

"Okay, look, this isn't helping," I allowed my Ki to dissipate and reach a level of calm.

I looked at Akira as he scowled at me and tried to think of a solution. Whether I liked it or not, we were stuck together: in class working as partners, as Shinobi on future missions, and as people living in the same village. This power struggle between us couldn't keep on. Somehow we had to call a truce and learn to work together. Yamamoto sensei did say that if Akira and I could learn to work and fight together we would be an unstoppable force. How was that ever going to happen with us constantly at each other's throats?

"Look, I'm sorry," I finally said and swallowed my pride.

He gaped at me. Surprise reflected in every feature of his

face. He stared at me in dumbfounded silence.

Seeing the response, I went on to say, "I'm sorry for dragging you along, I don't want you to get into trouble. I just want to do this, I-I guess to prove that I *can* do it, that I can do anything, and that I'm not weak."

"Nobody said you were weak," Akira snapped.

"Then what is it?"

"I don't know!"

Akira nudged me out of his way and started up the path to the right, pulling roughly on the long chain. I followed without a struggle, especially since this was the way I wanted to go in the first place.

"You and I used to get along when we were kids. What happened?" I said, trailing slightly behind him.

"I don't know."

"Sure you do. Your dad yelled at you the other day about fighting with some boy."

Akira suddenly wheeled around. "Shut up! You don't know anything about it!" He then turned his back on me and trudged up the path again.

"Yes I do," I said softly. "I heard him yell at you in Madam Yukia's shop the other day. He slapped you. It sounded like he was mad at you because of me."

That must've struck a nerve for Akira's anger came to a boil. He whirled around with his left fist up, aiming for my face. "Ahhhh!" he screamed and used his body's momentum to drive the punch with all his might.

I quickly ducked just as Akira's fist slammed into the tree behind me. The punch actually released the sound of a small blast and left a dent where he struck, sending shards of bark scattering in all directions. Strangely enough, Akira didn't hurt his hand in the least. Instead, he placed his hand on the tree and leaned heavily on the trunk, panting, upset and hung his head.

"It's all your fault. It's all your fault," he said softly, his voice wavering.

"What is?" I felt like I may have broken through the emotional barrier. "Dude, I have no idea what you're talking about or what I've done to upset you so much." When Akira didn't answer right away I pushed the issue. "When we were little I used to invite you to play ball with me. When the bullies wouldn't let you sit where you wanted at lunch time I would call you over to sit with me. We used to build sand castles together, remember?"

"And shortly after that you started showing off your abilities," Akira raised his head and glared at me; face red and eyes rimmed with tears.

"What abilities? I'm no different from the other kids!" I knew now that this was a lie, but I didn't want to tell him what I experienced.

"Yes you are – and my father noticed it and wanted me to be just like you for the family honor. He pushed me and pushed me. He even set up a special training playground in our backyard and drilled me to death. It wasn't fun anymore! And every time I couldn't jump like you, do flips like you, or do anything else that you could do, he spanked me. Pretty soon the punishments changed from spanking a child to full fledged beatings the older I got!"

I was speechless, I didn't quite know what to say, and after a brief moment said, "I'm sorry, Akira. I had no idea."

"That's because he made sure not to touch my face," He sniffed as tears streamed down his cheeks.

"Why didn't you tell someone?"

"And bring more shame on my family?" Akira turned away, wiped his face with the back of his hand. "I said nothing because in my father's eyes I brought enough shame on our family."

"Well, for what it's worth, I don't have any special abilities. I'm just a normal guy. What I do is just natural to me. I can't help that I can do what I do. That's just me and I wish all of you guys would chill out and accept me...for...me."

Once again, Akira started to walk up the path, wiping his face and not looking at me. I guessed he was lost in an emotional turmoil, remembering our innocent past yet dealing with the painful present. I felt now would be a good time and try to lighten the mood.

"Speaking of abilities, did you see what you did to that tree back there? It was like *wham!* and it exploded like *whoosh!* and tree parts went everywhere. Now that's power."

Akira came to an abrupt halt and turned his head to look at me skeptically. I gave him a quirky smile.

"Look, I don't want to fight with you anymore. It's not my fault your father wants you to be like me. That's not realistic. He has to accept you for you. You've got a lot of excellent qualities: you're a powerful fighter, excellent at close-range, you're fast and never give up. You and I would make a great Shinobi team."

"But you have Hikaru as a friend."

"You can never have too many friends," I said quietly, not understanding his reasoning. "Besides, Hikaru wouldn't mind if you hung out with us. He only has a problem with you because you have a problem with me."

Without waiting for a response I took the lead and moved up the path a bit faster now that the sun had begun to set.

We continued to walk in silence for another twenty minutes. The landscape changed; the trees were sparse and the ground became more boulders than soil.

"I told you we took the wrong way," Akira said, his voice sounding lighter and not as angry.

"The mill should just be around that rocky peak. It sits next to the waterfall, so we have to be going the right way," I used my Life Force Energy and lightly balanced myself on the wet rocks.

"We should keep our voices down, too," Akira suggested.

"Why?"

"Because of the mountain spirits, the trolls, they hate visitors," Akira now took the lead and found man-made stone steps embedded in the ground. "I hear they're seven feet tall, with arms thick like trees. They've got nasty tempers, worse than tengu's. Most of the ninja that come through here travel in silence, not touching the ground or disturbing nature. You never know where the trolls are because they blend in with the rocks, the trees, the soil - just everywhere."

"For all the shouting we've been doing the whole time I guess we've been pretty lucky," I said with a pleasant look on my face.

Just at that moment a rustle came from behind a tree off to our left. We turned around, dropped into a fighting stance the best we could with our left and right wrists cuffed together. Akira pulled out a kama from his sash, while I reached slowly over my head and unsnapped the strap holding my katana in their sheaths. I pulled out one of the beautiful swords without hesitation and held it in my right hand.

The rustling came again, this time from behind a crop of bushes next to a tree. What ever it was, it was moving closer. I looked at Akira and motioned with my eyes and a slight nod of my head that we should take cover. Akira nodded toward a large rock. The rustling continued, this time accompanied by grunts and snorts. Closer and closer it came, the bushes shook from the unseen force, but no footsteps were heard. We silently moved, but forgot that we were cuffed together. I went to the right and Akira went to the left, jerking us to a painful stop, the cuffs once again cutting into our wrists. Our eyes met, full of frustration, but I sighed and nodded for Akira to go first. Without hesitation,

Akira turned and swiftly moved up the bank and around the rock. I followed, staying close and moving as a unit. We ducked low, peered over the rock, and waited for the groaning monster to show its face.

The bushes shook even more, and the trees seemed to sway, whatever it was it seemed big, and was getting closer. My mouth had gone dry, my heart hammered inside my chest, and I felt an emotional electricity from Akira that told me he must be as nervous as I was. I readied my sword; Akira raised his kama. We were anxious for the battle to begin, to release our tension and get the fight over with. Closer it came, then, suddenly, a squirrel broke through the bushes with a small wild boar chasing after it. We sighed in relief at the sight of the two small animals, the squirrel racing around like mad and the boar frustrated and trying to run it over. Just as sudden as they appeared, the creatures quickly disappeared down the mountain path.

"Tsk, what a waste of time," Akira muttered, somewhat disappointed.

"Well, at least it wasn't a troll, or something," I said, feeling very foolish.

Moments later we came upon the old watermill. It was four stories high, a massive old wooden structure that towered over the boulders and trees, seemingly embedded into the mountain itself. It sat so close to the waterfall that I could feel a slight splash of water as we approached what looked like the front entrance.

I marveled at the size of the old building and was surprised to see the huge water wheel still turning from the force of the falls, creaking and moaning from its own movement.

The first thing I saw upon entering the building was the massive gears and wooden posts that turned in a continuous motion. It was once used to grind up wheat, barley and other items poured into the shaft above. Or, as Kenji said in his story, they ground up the body of the homeless man. I found myself actually looking to see if there were still tell-tale signs of blood smears on the gears.

"Wow," I said, "Pretty cool, huh?"

"Let's check the place out before it gets too dark," Akira suggested, his icy demeanor staring to melt slightly.

We climbed the flight of steps, finding nothing on the second, third, or fourth levels other than a few large barrels for water or grain and empty sacks draped over posts. We returned to the lower level.

"Well, it gets cold up here at night, so we need to build a fire," I spied a large square hole in the floor. The remnants of burnt wood still lingered.

It didn't take us long to build a fire and, thanks to the many times we stayed in the woods as kids, we had a natural sense of our surroundings, the sights, smells and sounds of the forest, as well as what was to be expected in the dark. As young ninja, we had learned at an early age to welcome the dark, to not be afraid and to use it as an ally. Taking advantage of a bad situation, learning to manipulate your surroundings and use what's at your disposal was all part of ninja survival. So, here we were, at the old mill, spending the night on a stupid dare because I wanted to prove something. We sat side by side near the fire, neither saying a word. An owl hooted outside in a nearby tree.

"I didn't bring a blanket. Did you?" I said breaking the silence.

At first he didn't answer; acting as if he talking to me was a problem. Then he finally said, "Didn't think about it."

"It's too dark to go out and look for something to eat," I said.

Akira poked the fire with a stick. "We'll just tough it out, like we've been trained to do."

I kept the small talk going in the hopes of breaking through his defenses more. "We shouldn't fall asleep for too long. We need to get to weapons class by five in the morning," I reminded him.

"Okay, we'll take turns sleeping while the other keeps watch," Akira suggested.

"We still need to get these off," I said, holding up my wrist.

He starred blankly for a moment then softened. "I have a feeling we'll have to show this to Master Katsumi." Akira gave a soft snort. "He'll probably get a laugh out of this one." The comment reminded me what Master Katsumi did to my sister and her rival so they would stop fighting and learn to get along.

We sat in silence for a moment then I said, "Do you think there really are trolls in these mountains?" I found it a bit unbelievable, yet understood that the trolls could actually be a metaphor for the earth spirits and not an actual being. Then again, there were entirely too many eye-witness accounts to dismiss the idea of their existence.

Akira released a sigh of defeat, a signal that he knew I was going to keep talking until he stopped being a prick to me. "That's what I've heard, and not just stories from the elders, but from grown men. Some of those men used to work up here."

He was still answering my questions and comments and that meant he was giving in and allowing the hatred toward me to subside.

"Well, so far we've been lucky."

Just then the wind picked up, the old mill creaked and groaned, a loose board knocked gently against the side of the building somewhere upstairs, and a faint huffing, panting sound could be heard in the distance. I ignored it, not about to let fear take control, and blew it off as just the wind moaning through the boulders and trees.

6

Unwelcome Visitors

The evening rolled on and it was my turn to be on watch. Akira leaned against a wall, his head to the side, snoring lightly. I sat cross-legged close to the fire and poked it with a stick to keep it blazing. The night had become very cold since the sun went down and I shivered, even while sitting near to the fire. I wished I had worn my gi instead of a thin T-shirt with my black workout pants and tabi boots.

I can do this, I thought. *A ninja must be able to function in extreme environments, with little or no food, no water, no sleep and possibly no shelter.*

I let out a heavy sigh and focused my attention to the sounds surrounding the mill. An owl continued to hoot and screech, a cool breeze whipped around the building and seeped through cracks in the wood, branches of the trees hit together, and the roar of the waterfall kept up its steady pace rushing over the rocks and turning the massive, old waterwheel.

Nothing suspicious. Everything seems as it should be, I thought.

I then turned my attention inward. The fire crackled cheerfully, Akira snored and drooled on his own shoulder, the gears creaked and groaned as they turned, and from time to time the floorboards overhead would pop and make sounds like someone was walking around.

It's just from the wood cooling down, I told myself. *Our house does the same thing. The sun warms up the wood, making it expand, and then the night cools it down, making it contract.*

I sighed and relaxed, tilting my head from side to side to stretch my neck. Then, from overhead, there suddenly came a different sound, one of soft thumping, dragging and scraping.

That's not the wood popping, I thought. My pulse raced and my body tensed.

I scooted over to Akira.

"Akira," I whispered and shook his knee. "Wake up."

Akira woke with a start, kama suddenly in his hand.

"What the..."

I clapped my hand over Akira's mouth then placed a finger to my own lips to show that he needed to be quiet. I then motioned with my eyes to the floor above. Akira followed my gaze, tensed at the sound of soft thumping, and nodded understanding. I then removed my hand from his mouth, noticed the drool and wiped my hand on Akira's shirt. He scowled. I ignored him and helped him to his feet. We kept low in a crouched position as Akira readied his kama and I wasted no time pulling out one red-handled katana; the blade glinted in the moonlight.

The thumping sound was joined by multiple thumping sounds, resonating all over the three levels above us, moving down the steps and knocking over empty barrels.

Akira and I stayed low, looked at each other questioningly and summed up that the only way anyone could've gotten upstairs without us noticing was through an open window on the fourth floor. However, from our earlier investigation of the building, the only way through one of those windows was to climb a tree and jump in. Whatever was walking around sounded big, too big to get in through the windows, and the deep grunting sounds made by the intruder had me imagining it was something thick and large.

Akira tapped me on the leg and pointed to a dark shadowy spot under the steps. I agreed and we moved swiftly and silently to the designated area. From this vantage point, we could see through the open slats at what was coming down the steps and slash its tendons, if need be, rendering it unable to attack. We didn't have to wait long before the intruder made its appearance.

A hulking mass came plodding down the steps to ground level. It walked hunched over, yet it was very tall, and carried a massively thick club with spikes protruding all around the tip. It was furry with long hair hanging from under and along its arms, sides and back. The feet were huge, with thick pads on the bottom and long dirty toenails that clicked and scraped the floorboards. The large hands that held the club were almost identical to the feet. What caught our attention before any of the physical characteristics was the smell – pungent and relentless, like a cross between wet dog and a cow pen. We scrunched up our noses and made gestures to each other. Akira actually smiled at my actions.

The creature stopped halfway down the steps and looked around. It sniffed the air and grunted; an odd gurgling sound vibrated from its throat. Suddenly, another creature of equal height and build accompanied it. Together they sniffed the air.

I held my sword sideways in front of Akira's and my body, keeping it steady and on guard. Akira fidgeted behind me, nervously flipping his kama around his left hand and keeping an eye on the creatures.

Finally a third creature came down the steps, pushing the other two out of the way. This one wore a tattered loincloth and leather armbands laced at the wrists. It wasn't until all three were on ground level and walking around that we got a good look at their faces in the firelight. They had large protruding foreheads that housed tiny red eyes, their noses were flattened and crooked, and their lower lips and jaws protruded showing off slimy, yellowed tusks. They were quite intimidating and we shrank back, blending in with the shadows, yet never taking our eyes off of the trolls.

The troll with the armbands pushed the other two out of his way as he stomped around the room, sniffing and becoming agitated. He went from one corner to the next, stopping and scanning the surroundings. He gurgled in his throat; the other two did the same. They snorted and grumbled, then split up and walked around opposite sides of the stairs, heading for the dark empty spot where we hid.

Out of fear, I reached back and latched onto Akira's shirt, pulling some chest hair by accident. Akira winced and pried my hand away. The cuff chain jangled slightly, and it was enough to draw the troll's attention.

The troll leader plodded under the stairs and squinted its tiny red eyes, trying to see into the darkness. Akira and I recoiled and pressed our backs against the wall. Fear gripped our hearts; we tried our best to keep our breath under control. The troll sniffed the air and lowered his head. A massive hand swiped at the darkness as it tried to find the strange odor that annoyed it so much. Finally, unable to take the frustration, the troll released a mighty roar, raised a spiked club high above his head and brought it down where we were hiding.

We sprang into action; unfortunately we went in opposite directions. The cuff chain pulled taut, jerked us to a halt and our feet flew out from under us. We landed on our backs and rolled to our sides. Akira and I were lucky the spiked club landed just in front of us. The troll must've seen our movement as we scrambled to our feet and backed up. It swiped a hand through the air again and grabbed the chain that connected us. He roared as he lifted us above his head; with all his might he threw us back to the floor. I landed on my side and felt a sharp pain in my ribs. Akira did a face plant on the floorboards, but quickly got up and looked at me. He had a bloody nose.

The troll bellowed again and reached for us. Answering bellows echoed along the walls as other trolls joined the hunt.

"We need to move as one," I shouted over the noise. "This way!"

With my weapon I slashed at the creature's lower leg and it rose up in pain. The other two trolls lumbered closer to see what the matter was and noticed our movements. They also became agitated and drew their clubs over their heads.

Akira and I stayed low to the ground. As our training took over, we moved together, avoiding the clubs that smashed to the floor. We ran around the steps, weaving in and out of the troll's legs, and summarized that the troll's eyesight was bad, but their sense of smell was excellent. The creatures would pin-point us soon if we didn't do something.

We approached one of the subordinate trolls. Akira crouched low, on the balls of his feet, and gathered Ki to his legs. As soon as the creature turned to face him, Akira sprang up, slashed first at the creature's side, and then close to where the kidneys would be on the back. The troll shrieked as she slashed at him with long, dirty claws and my movements on the ground distracted the creature enough for Akira to latch onto her long hair and swing to the ground.

The leader turned swiftly, swinging his club with so much force he took out the entire stair. Splintered wood flew in every direction and the troll roared in anger that he had missed us. Now on the ground, Akira tucked his kama into his sash, grabbed onto the cuff on his wrist and started to spin in a circle. I ran around him, faster and faster we went until I was air-born. My feet hit one section of the wall and I ran with my swords at the ready. I slashed at the leader five times before I flipped to land on the floor. The troll let out a blood-curdling howl.

The third troll decided to come to the rescue, but Akira had other ideas. He pulled out a few throwing stars and whipped them at the troll's lower legs. The creature screamed as they struck, one, two, three, up the side of his leg. Akira sprang into a dive roll and I moved with him. Side-by-side and completely in sync, we zigzagged back and forth until we were directly below the troll. I landed on one knee, the other positioned like a step, as Akira vaulted off my leg and slashed the troll across his neck with his kama.

Terrified of the tiny, horrible, biting things that hurt them, the trolls roared and turned to run. They slammed into the side of the building, smashed down a portion of the wall, and fell over each other. In their haste, they slipped on the wet rocks near the falls and fell in.

Akira and I stepped out into the fresh morning air and watched them.

I favored my side and watched the creatures thrash in the churning water. "I didn't think trolls liked the water."

"They don't," Akira said stifling a chuckle and wiped his bloody nose on his arm.

We watched until the trolls were washed down river and their cries of anguish died out.

"Whew! What a night, huh?" Akira slapped me on the shoulder in a friendly manner.

"Aren't you glad you came along?"

"Did I have a choice?"

Moments later, the first pink rays of light started to show over the treetops, the birds started to sing and the world began to wake.

"Come on, we better get going or we'll be late for class,"
Akira jerked the cuffs and grinned.

Without another word we went inside the mill, put out the
fire, got a drink from the river and headed back down the mountain path. Forty-five minutes later we emerged through the dense
thicket of trees that lined our village. Sitting on a fallen tree was
Mayumi. She held my books, gym bag and clutched something
in her hand.

"Looks who's waiting for you," Akira said quietly and
bumped my hand with the back of his.

"Hey guys," Mayumi rushed up to us. "Class is going to start
in thirty minutes, so we better get moving."

She stood on her toes and gave me a quick kiss on the cheek.

"You really did keep my stuff, huh?" I said.

"Yeah. I thought it would be best so I could back you up this
morning." She paused and stared into my face dreamily then
blinked and said, "Oh, here, I brought this," Mayumi produced
a tiny key, "I thought you'd might like to get those cuffs off."

Akira and I looked at the key and held our hands up so she
could unlock the cuffs.

"Where'd you find it?" Akira watched Mayumi slip the key
into the keyhole and unlock each cuff.

"Actually, Haru found it shortly after you guys left. It was in
his shoe the whole time," Mayumi offered a lopsided grin.

I snorted, slowly shook my head, and rubbed my wrist where
the cuff had repeatedly cut into it. I took my schoolbooks and
gym bag from Mayumi, kissed her on the cheek and said,
"Thanks for being here. It means a lot."

Mayumi blushed and looked at me shyly. We lost ourselves
in the moment, forgetting that Akira was standing next to us
watching.

"Oh, yeah, I almost forgot. Here, Akira, this is if for you," she tore her eyes away from me and handed him a tablet, pen and her math book. "You can use these this morning until you can go home and get your stuff. You can just give the book back later."

"She's sharp and on the ball," Akira said to me with a slight smile then to Mayumi he said, "Thanks. I appreciate it."

He walked off ahead of us, stuffing the handcuffs in the pouch on his hip.

"Wow, what a difference," Mayumi said completely shocked as she watched Akira head for weapons class ahead of us. "What'd you do, beat him senseless?"

7

By Special Invitation Only

Classes were over by two o'clock and I wandered home alone. Yet deep inside I didn't feel alone at all and I walked with a little spring in my step. My heart felt lighter and I didn't feel the burning rage in my gut as much. That was most likely because the fighting with Akira was over. Remembering last night, I allowed a little smile to pass over my lips, but winced and reached for my side. It was quite obvious I cracked a rib when the troll slammed me to the ground. It was all I could do to hide the fact from everyone during my classes, and I didn't want to go to the infirmary to get it looked at. One of the nurses would surely tell Uncle. I couldn't wrap my sides with bandages because that only restricts breathing. I couldn't do anything but be careful. How long would I be able to keep it hidden?

This was the new dilemma I found myself in. I also had mixed emotions about last night and the past happenings of the last few days. My truce with Akira felt great yet a little odd. The situation with Hikaru over Mayumi and that my best friend was possibly afraid of me still played heavy on my mind, as well as receiving a Dragon Stone. But the biggest worry was this whole crazy business about something strange taking over my body, living off my anger and controlling me. I seemed that as long as I stayed calm I didn't hear it in my head or feel its presence. Keeping it ,and my anger, suppressed was always a challenge. The question rose about needing its help to fight. I fought just fine without it in the old mill, but not when I was faced with death from Shi'tori.

This is it, I thought. *I've got to sit down with Uncle and get some answers. I can't keep putting this off anymore.*

I cut through a few backyards and came very close to a pagoda near a small pond with weeping cherry trees all around. It was the very one where Shi'tori threatened my life. There, sitting alone on the steps with a book was Morgan.

"Hey Duncan," Morgan muttered as I passed by, not really looking up from his book.

"Hey," I said, slowing down but not really stopping.

"How'd things go last night?" Morgan said, casually.

That got my attention. I stopped, turned and walked over to him, and then put my foot on a step and leaned on my knee. "How'd you know about that?"

Morgan looked up from his book, our eyes met, and though his long bangs were hiding much of his face I could tell he was sporting a sly grin. The look alone was his answer.

"Oh, never mind," I said after a brief pause. "It went...uh... good, I guess."

I turned to leave, but Morgan's next question took me by surprise.

"Have any trouble with trolls?" He looked back at his book and slowly turned a page. "I hear they hang out around the old watermill."

"A-a little," I looked at him from over my shoulder. There

was no way he could know. How could he have known? I was now very suspicious. "How? Um...how are you getting this information?"

"I may not be a fighter like you and the other guys...but I have my methods." Morgan met my stare, held it, and then finally shrugged before looking away, "I'm just saying."

For as strange as Morgan was, it was apparent that he was a great spy and excellent at stealth. It was a trait most people took years to master and one that would be highly desirable on a mission.

"Oh, w-well, that's pretty cool...do me a favor and just make sure you're on my team someday, okay?" I grinned, turned away and walked towards home.

I didn't get very far when I noticed Kikaku off in the distance walking very fast and glancing over his shoulders. He was nervous, even twitchy, and his actions piqued my curiosity. All the talk about Kikaku running off alone and sneaking around late at night floated to mind. I hung back, melting into the shadows of a building, and watched him a bit longer. He broke into a light jog and rounded a corner. Now was my chance.

I stole from my hiding place and jogged to catch up, yet stayed close to buildings and trees as I went. I rounded the corner and stopped, scanning the area for Kikaku. He took a sharp left through a grove of trees. I pursued. I stayed low and silent as I slinked several feet behind, making sure not to step on a stick or crunch a pinecone. The least little sound would alarm him and I knew Kikaku would turn on me in an instant. My pulse raced as I kept up the pace, and thoughts of discovering Kikaku's little secret fueled the excitement brewing in my chest. With a sudden burst of speed he took off, looking like a blur as he zipped through trees and brush. It was a simple technique, one we learned in our pre-teens, and it was effortless for me to execute the same. But it wasn't easy trying to keep up. Kikaku had an advantage on me: his skill and age.

He pulled ahead, cleared the trees and disappeared.

"Damn!" I stopped at the tree line and scanned the area. Kikaku was nowhere in sight. Unfortunately, I found myself at the boundaries of the Black Dragon Squad's training area and barracks. If I were found out I was sure there would be no mercy for the ass-kicking they'd give me, so I hung back and blended in with the shadows.

I suspected Kikaku went inside the barracks, but he had to come out some time. And I knew that since he was only a pre-Black Dragon he didn't live in the barracks yet. He still lived at home until he passed the Final Trials. When he was finished inside the barracks he would come out and I would be waiting.

I lounged high in the branches of a tree and kept my sights on the Black Dragon Barracks. Thirty minutes later the door slid open and Kikaku emerged with Captain Yoshida on his heels grumbling and shaking the handle of a kuni at him. I couldn't hear what was being said, but it didn't sound good. Kikaku was definitely getting a lecture.

I rose up to a squat, favoring my ribs while trying to be careful. During the time I had been waiting in the tree my body had started to stiffen up. Focusing my mind and relaxing helped me channel my Ki. It lent strength to my sore muscles and allowed me to be ready to spring into action as I watched Kikaku pass under me. Silent as a mountain lion I dropped to the ground and pursued him. My hopes rose at the thought of catching him doing something unethical, meeting someone in secret and busting him red-handed. Unfortunately all the excitement fizzled out the moment he approached his house and went inside. His adoptive parents greeted him; a kiss on the cheek from his mother and his father handed him a basket of potatoes. The door shut and my pursuit was over. Dead end.

I released a sigh of defeat, but decided I wasn't going to give up. As I headed home I mulled things over in my mind. There were too many strange things that had happened over the past month and they all involved Kikaku in some way. Shi'tori was one of them. She had known Kikaku intimately, which was odd since she had only been in our village for two days before I killed her. How does someone get so intimate with a stranger in two days? It was obvious to me that she already knew him ahead of time. Plus she was a Shimoshuki. The question of how Kikaku and Shi'tori met seemed like a strange situation. Our two clans never mingled and the only thing that did make sense was, perhaps, they came upon a chance meeting in the forest and fell in love. Yeah, right. But once they found out they were from rival clans they should've ended it, right? Maybe they liked each other so much that they just didn't care and carried on their love affair in secret.

Then only a week after I killed Shi'tori talk among the other teens about Kikaku running off alone late at night started to circulate. Was he out looking for her at their secret meeting place? Did he have another lover lined up already, or was it for another reason? Whatever it was, Captain Yoshida may have gotten wind of it. That reaming-out he gave Kikaku today wasn't just for his health. Something was up, that much was certain. Either Kikaku wasn't following orders, or the captain asked him about the late night rendezvous and didn't get the answer he wanted to hear.

Thinking about this whole mess gave me a headache. Nothing made sense, but I was going to find out the truth and for a ninja the possibilities were endless. It all depended on how you played the game.

I continued on my way, home was very close now and so was

the weapons training area. Master Katsumi was lounging in his chair outside the weapons shack.

"Duncan!" Master Katsumi waved me over.

"Great, what'd I do wrong now?" I muttered to myself.

Inside I grumbled, but on the outside I approached the weapons master with the greatest respect. I actually liked Master Katsumi, regardless of how tough of a sensei he could be. And the fact that he knew something about me that I didn't understand intrigued me all the more.

"Yes, sensei?" I bowed slightly as I stopped in front of him.

"Duncan, I'm so glad you happened to be walking by." I knew that wasn't the truth even though he smiled and set the tone of his voice so it did sound true. "I've been talking to your uncle about your performance..."

"I haven't lost my temper in class, sensei, and I've really been trying..."

"Don't interrupt! I didn't call you over here to reprimand you. I want to tell you that you're doing a fine job, you're above your peers, and I've expressed this to Tou-Pang." He paused and. When I didn't respond he plunged on. "We feel that you need further training, training you won't get until you go into the Black Dragon Squad."

"Am I being tried for the squad?" I said, excitement building in my gut.

"No, no, nothing like that – at least not yet. No, what you really need is some one-on-one training; more hard-core, advanced stuff."

This must be what Captain Yoshida and Master Katsumi were talking about earlier - special training. Captain Yoshida said he wanted me early, like this year; I'd be the youngest ever to enter the Black Dragon Squad. I felt a little deflated that I wasn't being tried for the squad right now. However, if that wasn't the case, this special training made me suspicious of the real reason behind the decision. I wasn't going to argue about the one-on-one training. It would only make me better, stronger and faster, which was another thing I strived for. And maybe, just maybe, this special training would help me tap into my special elemental energies and fighting style.

"What will I be doing? Who will I work with? When do I start?" I fired off the string of questions faster than Master Katsumi could answer.

"You'll be working with me and we start in two weeks. We'll meet here at five o'clock in the evening. Bring all weapons and be ready to hit the forest. We'll work well into the night," Master Katsumi's tone told me there was no room for argument.

"Okay, sounds great! Is there anything else I need to know?"

"Only one thing, how quickly you learn will depend on how long I stay with you."

"Oh?" I said.

"Once you reach a certain point in your training, where I can no longer teach you, I will then hand you off to another trainer. I'll let you know when that time comes, but don't worry about it now."

My head was swimming with the possibilities of who this other trainer could be. Who else among the sensei in our village could help bring out that powerful life force, allowing me to harness the energy and fuse it with my weapon?

"And Duncan, this training is not to be discussed with anyone...understand? No one." He stood and placed a massive hand on my shoulder. "This is all part of being a Shinobi – secrecy and trust. The Black Dragon Squad members do it all the time. They come and go, in and out of the village, no one really sees them – I know you've noticed. You spy on them all the time. Their Trials are secret, they stay a close knit group, knowing each other's private problems, yet not speaking about them, and they go on missions all the time completely unnoticed by our people."

Everything Master Katsumi said was true; the Squad was very mysterious, they rarely talked to people in the village and, if they did, you didn't know about it. No one knew what kind of missions they went on, when they went, or how things turned out. I'd been tempted many times to follow them and find out exactly what went on, but I had always gotten distracted and missed the opportunities. Now that this additional training was going to start, I felt a chance might come up again. Besides, I beat a tengu and faced monstrous trolls, tracking a Black Dragon Squad member to see where he went may not be so hard after all.

"Do you understand what I'm saying?" Master Katsumi's voice broke into my thoughts.

"Yes, sensei."

"Good. See you in the morning for weapons class." The weapons master walked away; his manner stated that he was satisfied with our talk.

My heart raced as I turned and continued to walk home. This is what I'd been waiting for; a chance to advance in skill, to move forward. Perhaps Master Katsumi wasn't afraid of me or of my anger, or what would happen while working with me and if I lost control? It was clear to me that my anger issue had a lot to do with my abilities. But how far could I go with it? Was the voice in my head real, or was I making it up? When it was quiet, when I had control and I didn't hear it for a long time, that's when it seemed like it was all made up. But when I totally lost myself and allowed it to take over, that's when it became more real and very scary.

There had to be a reason I had this special thing. There was always a reason for everything. Just like my Dragon Stone. Was there a reason for the tengu to give me the Dragon Stone, or was that just a fluke thing? Maybe the tengu could sense the thing inside me and that's why I was chosen?

I sighed and shook my head. Nothing made sense, but maybe Uncle would have some answers. This special training would only increase my chances of being accepted into the squad. The downfall was that it would take away my free time with Hikaru and Mayumi and I couldn't even tell them why I was going to be too busy to hang out in the evenings.

It didn't matter, though. When a ninja lied it was only the truth rearranged, which didn't make it a lie at all. I'd have to worry about it when confronted, but right now I had my sights set on Kikaku. I was going to find out what he was up to, even if it cost me more cracked ribs.

8

Secret Rendezvous

I waited until late into the night, after Uncle was sound asleep, to sneak out of the house. Dressed in black, I packed my pouch with stars, kuni and essential items needed for tracking and protection. I removed a few floorboards in my closet to reveal one of the many escape tunnels, grabbed my swords, jumped in and emerged in the forest not far from the house. Blending with the night shadows I slipped silently through town and stopped close to Kikaku's house. It was quiet as I approached his bedroom window and chanced a peek inside. He wasn't in his bed, which meant he had already left.

I spat a silent curse. I'd waited too long. He could be anywhere by now. I looked around and scanned the trees. I tried to get my enhanced eyesight and hearing to work, but couldn't, and summed up that it might only work under extremely stressful circumstances. As fate would have it I caught movement out of the corner of my eye. In the distance a shadow moved through the trees and deeper into the forest. Maybe I didn't miss him after all?

I followed at a safe distance, yet never lost track of the shadow. When he slowed down, so did I; when he changed directions, I waited a heartbeat before doing the same. He led me far from the village, over the river that connected to the waterfall and out toward the fields. As I zipped through the trees I noticed another shadow off to my right. It went in a different direction, more towards the waterfall and the old mill. Had I been found out? Was I being surrounded? Gathering Ki in my thighs I vaulted into the trees for protection and concealment, still following at a safe distance and getting a better view of my impending situation.

The shadow that I felt was Kikaku paused behind a boulder, looked around, and then walked out into a small open area. I watched from my perch, high in a nearby tree. Seconds ticked by. He stood there, waiting. The moon was waning; the light was dim so I couldn't get a good look at my target. It was Kikaku, I was sure of it; I mean, it had to be. His bed was empty; gossip of him running off alone late at night had been circulating for the past two weeks, so I couldn't be wrong.

Another shadow came out of the trees and brush. Kikaku's back was to him, seemingly not paying attention. The newcomer rushed forward; his katana blade flashed in the moonlight as he slashed for whom I felt was Kikaku. The shadow Kikaku drew his sword as he spun to face his foe. Steel against steel rang out in the night. They froze and held each other's gaze. Paused. Then relaxed.

"It's about time," the attacker said, his voice deep and droning, the outline of his body made him look like a hulking mass. "I've been waiting for a while now."

"I told you I'd be here," the other said.

Wait a minute. That voice. It's a little different, yet sounded like Kikaku. No, no, I was sure it was Kikaku. I had to be careful. I couldn't wrongfully accuse someone. I had to be absolutely sure. That's how the Dragons conducted themselves and if I wanted to be one of them someday I had to maintain that mindset. If Kikaku was doing something wrong he had to be brought to justice. Now, who this other guy was, well, I'd just have to find out - somehow.

"Did you bring it?" Deep Droning Voice said.

"Yeah, yeah, I told you I would." Shadow Kikaku pulled out what looked like a folded piece of paper from his gi and went to hand it over.

Deep Droning Voice reached for it, but Shadow Kikaku drew his hand back.

"Oh no ya don't. Payment first," Shadow Kikaku demanded, suddenly holding a kuni at the other man's throat.

They stared at each other for a long moment. I shifted my position slightly in the tree as I watched. Finally the man slowly reached into his gi, never taking his eyes off Shadow Kikaku, and pulled out a wrapped item. Shadow Kikaku pressed the blade into the man's neck; a reaction of mistrust. When the wrapped item was set in the open, both relaxed, even laughed a little and the tension between them melted.

"Here you go," Deep Droning Voice said, "Five hundred big ones, as promised." He handed the bundle to Shadow Kikaku who, in turn, handed him the paper.

"And here's my end of the bargain, but it wasn't easy."

They looked over their prizes in silence.

"I still can't believe some foreigner is interested in this stuff," Shadow Kikaku stuffed the wad of money in his gi.

"Lord Zahn is a great man, with a great vision for all of humanity. What he has in mind for the entire world will put everyone, of every nation on the same level," Deep Droning Voice said.

I snorted to myself and shook my head. *This guy sounds like he plans on taking over the world and restoring a new order*, I thought.

"Whatever," Kikaku waved off the comment then paused, stiffened and scanned the trees.

The big guy took notice, pulled out his katana and dropped low to the ground, scanning the trees, also.

Had I been found out? That second shadow, had it returned? Had it been watching me while I was observing the exchange, plotting and planning to silence me? I stayed low on the branch high in the tree and watched the night, waiting for someone to come out of the dark and attack me. My heart hammered in my chest; I struggled to keep my breathing under control. Even the best ninja can locate an enemy just by listening for his breathing and I wouldn't put it past these guys to zero in on me in a matter of seconds.

This slight distraction was my downfall and I was so busy scanning the night that I didn't notice the big guy slip into the shadows and disappear until it was too late. From out of the darkness he barreled into me with the force of a linebacker and slammed me into the trunk of the tree. The entire tree shook, leaves fluttered to the ground and I struggled to release his grip from around my neck. Drawing my knees to my chest I kicked him and knocked him backwards. He staggered, lost his footing and fell. I heard him land on the ground with a *whump!* I did a back handspring to my feet, drew one dragon sword and looked around. He was gone and so was Shadow Kikaku. Damn!

Effortlessly I dropped to the ground only to be attacked by the big guy once more.

"How much did you hear?" he demanded, landing a front snap kick to my stomach.

I absorbed the kick and executed a back handspring away from him, landed on my feet and back rolled further into the open area where he and Shadow Kikaku had been conducting business just a moment ago. I pulled out my other sword, stayed low and waited for his next move.

He stepped into the dim moonlight and I recognized him immediately. I could never forget this guy. It was one of the Shimoshuki that had attacked me and Hikaru several weeks ago.

"Answer me! How much did you hear?"

When I still didn't answer he charged at me and I met him head-on. He brought his blade down in an overhead slash. I crossed my swords in an X and blocked. Our blades clashed, and their metallic ring resounded through the night. His weight bore down on me, forcing me to one knee. He grinned, his eyes wild. I circled our blades to the right, which released his hold, and rolled to the left, coming up to my feet. He didn't waste any time regaining himself.

"Should've killed you when I had the chance!" he shouted and held his blade sideways in front of him.

I wasn't exactly sure what he did next; I had never seen anything like it before. The Shimoshuki seemed to be channeling energy from his hands into the hilt of his sword and down the blade. The edges of the blade glowed and crackled with power as he gently ran one hand down to the tip. I took a step back not sure how to combat his next attack – whatever it might be.

He sliced the air and threw the energy off his blade and in my direction.

Panic seized me. I jumped out of the way as a tremendous bolt of energy whizzed across the ground, tearing up the earth and anything in its way, and dissipated once it went past.

"Can't handle my attack?" he gloated. "I call it suto-mu - storm blade." He slowly advanced on me. "I should've used it on you the last time we met, you little freak! Don't think I forgot what you did to the brothers in my clan."

He sliced his sword through the air once more and another bolt of energy came at me. I jumped to the side as it took out the tree behind me. When I looked up I noticed that his sword was suddenly back to normal and I assumed the energy was used up. I had to act, but before I even had a chance to stand he was on me, hacking crazily with his katana, using side-to-side and overhead strikes. It was all I could do to defend, never having a chance to counter attack. He elbowed me in the face several times, hacking as he went and then landed a direct punch in my face. Blood dripped from my nose as my knees buckled. Then my hands lost feeling and I dropped my swords and fell on my back. Seizing the opportunity he stomped on my chest and gloated.

"Ha! You're not so tough now are you, freak?" He leaned his weight on me and twisted his foot. My already sore and cracked rib screamed with pain, but I couldn't let him know that. Once an enemy knows your weakness, they'll use it against you.

Pain radiated through my chest as I grabbed his foot and tried to twist him off of me, but it was no use, he was too heavy. I grabbed one of my katana in an underhanded hold and slashed at his legs. He easily blocked. It was too simple with the position I was in. I couldn't get leverage to do any real damage and I was panicked. I spat blood and gritted my teeth; my breathing came in shallow gasps of pain. My cracked rib twisted under his weight and I was sure I now had a broken nose. Where was my Dragon Stone power when I needed it? Surely this was a dire situation where my stone would awaken and lend me the strength and knowledge to defeat my enemy, just like what happened to Captain Yoshida? Where was the help when I needed it?

Just ask...

That voice...just ask? That's what it said before, when I was battling Shi'tori and near death. I could never forget what happened then. But it doesn't have to be that devastating. I just want to get away from this guy.

Tell me...

Yes. I could do that. I closed my eyes for a moment and concentrated, using what I had learned in meditation training. *Lend me the strength,* I told the voice.

"Giving up, I see," the big guy said. I heard him adjust his katana with both hands and when I chanced a peek out of one eye I saw that he had raised it high, aiming the tip of the blade for my heart.

"Let him go!" A demanding voice came from out of the shadows and I recognized it immediately.

I opened my eyes and saw Shinji standing close by with his bow held ready for battle, a light orange glow of power emanating from the tips. It was a side of him I'd never seen before.

"Let me kill this one, and then I'll take care of you!" our mutual enemy sneered.

I had to do this, to summon my power, and it had to be now. Shinji could get killed and I had to protect him. As I closed my eyes once more a warm tingling sensation started in my gut and quickly radiated through my entire upper body. The sensation I felt was one of being *full* and *complete,* which may sound crazy, but I don't know any other way to describe it. Just then I snapped my eyes open and my enemy hesitated in mid-strike, as if to make out who I was. I concentrated the warm energy down my left arm to my dragon sword, willing it to make the dragon etched on the blade come to life. In the blink of an eye a slight blue flame enveloped my katana, pulsing with life, but deep in my mind I suddenly wanted death. I felt invincible, empowered, and it must've radiated from my body because the Shimoshuki drew back as if not sure how to proceed with his plan to run me through. This I used to my advantage.

With my newfound power I kicked my legs up, caught him behind the knees and rolled to the side. He flipped to the ground and I finally found the means to stand. Shinji rushed to my side, but stopped when I turned to look at him. He squinted at me in the dim moonlight and took a step back, and then gazed questioningly at my katana.

"Duncan?"

I turned away from him and fixed my gaze on my enemy. Determination filled my mind and I was set on getting rid of this human...this pest. As the big guy stood to face us I could feel his fear; the taste of it was ripe as it filtered through my skin. I raised my katana above my head and threw a rope of blue flame at the Shimoshuki. It shot out in three branches of energy, taking on the look of a claw, like the claw of the mighty dragon of the waterfall. And at that moment I decided to name it Dragon Claw. The blast was met by the suto-mu attack of the Shimoshuki and the two exploded into a brilliant light of energy; a shock wave of power blew in all directions. It quickly dissipated and the Shimoshuki was still standing, smiling triumphantly.

"I got this," Shinji said; twirling his bow above his head, power pulsing from the wood grain finish. He jumped and spun, then landed in a strong fighting stance as he sliced the air in front of him with one end of his bow, and then the other, faster than I had ever seen him move before. "Wolf's Bane!" he shouted. A swirl of orange light shot out from each end, criss-crossing each other in the air like scissors, dead center of the Shimoshuki's chest.

The big guy raised his katana and blocked the attack, seemingly trying to absorb it. He grunted and strained, digging the toes of his boots into the earth as the attack held firm, pulsating with power, and pushed into him. Finally he couldn't hold it any longer and the blast blew him back into the trees. Shinji and I held our ground. We waited. Was he finished? Movement under a pile of broken trees told us the Shimoshuki was still alive. He grunted and groaned and used the bent trees to pull himself up, panting in pain as shiny streaks of blood clung to his skin and dripped down one arm, but he wasn't finished fighting. With his right hand he summoned power, channeling it into his blade once again. I was ready for him this time. Where his blade seemed to run out of power after two strikes, mine did not, for it was connected to my very being. When he flung his suto-mu attack again I gathered my strength, focused, stepped in front of Shinji as a shield and cast my Dragon Claw attack.

The blasts of energy slammed into each other with so much force it blew back bushes, loosened boulders and bent trees. Shinji and I braced ourselves and held our ground. The blast subsided, but the energy from the attacks held firm, like two creatures locked in a death grip. To my amazement, I saw that my Claw had actually grasped the Shimoshuki's suto-mu energy bolt, latched on like it had a mind of its own. Perhaps it did? A slight smile of satisfaction touched the corner of my mouth and I channeled even more energy from my blade, down the length of the blue Dragon Claw, willing it to squeeze the life out of the suto-mu.

The Shimoshuki held tight to his katana, one hand over the other, his muscles bulging as his arms trembled under the strain of trying to control his attack and hold mine at bay. More blood dripped down his arm. The sight of it excited me. I pushed a bit more, willing my attack to finish him. The Shimoshuki cried out in agony, and fell to one knee as his katana slowly leaned toward his head. He couldn't hold my attack anymore and I willed him to die. I wanted death, the idea of it consumed me, to see a life snuffed out thrilled me and I couldn't control my desire. The raging energy inside of me wanted more, but the passive side knew this wasn't right. I tried to regain myself, to remember that I was a Shinobi of the Chiao Village. I was better than this guy; I couldn't kill him. Instead I should arrest him and catch Kikaku, bring them before the elders and watch them squirm. This idea appealed to my inner demon more and I opted for a different ending to the Shimoshuki.

I released a breath, focused my will, seemingly 'talking' to the Dragon Claw energy. In a flash, the energy from his attack dissipated, literally sucked into mine, and my Dragon Claw quickly retreated into my blade. All was quiet as the blue flames danced lightly around it like a soft caress. The only sound left was the Shimoshuki's scream of pain as he rose from his knees.

"What did you do?" he shouted, holding his katana in a lifeless hand. He staggered, leaned on a nearby tree and panted like he had run a marathon. He glared at me and struggled to stay upright. "You drained me! You took away my power! How could you do that? That's not even possible!" He retched and swooned and reached into his pouch for something.

"You're coming with us," Shinji said sternly. "Our authorities have some questions."

Shinji moved forward to capture him, but the Shimoshuki suddenly threw a smoke pellet at the ground. The thick swirling mist clouded our vision, but it was too late once it cleared. He had made his escape.

"Damn!" I spat. "I didn't even find out his name, or what he was doing out here with Kikaku."

"So, you were following him too?" Shinji said then pointed at me. "First of all...dude, what the hell happened to you? I couldn't believe it when I saw you change."

"Long story." I looked away, embarrassed yet hopeful as I felt a level of myself coming back.

"Wanna share?"

"Well, what about you? I never knew you could throw an attack like that, and so fast and so good!" I paused, breathed and tried to let my expanded blue energy relax, release and allow me to become normal again. Being with carefree Shinji would probably help. In between deep slow breaths I said, "You're old enough to go up for so many advanced things. Yet you waste your time goofing off with Masa. What's up with that?"

Let me stay...

The voice was insistent and I almost felt obligated, but I wasn't about to let it control me. I ignored it until its whisper couldn't be heard any longer. Besides, I didn't want to tell Shinji about it, he was already a bit freaked out by what he witnessed tonight.

He shrugged and said, "Long story, too."

"Well, we have some catching up to do," I clapped him on the shoulder and turned to walked away, paused and said, "Do me a favor. Don't tell anyone. It'll just be our secret. Okay?"

He cocked his head and said, "Sure. If that's the way you want it. I won't say anything."

"Thanks."

"That's what Shinobi do. That's what friends do. But don't you want to go after Kikauku and find out what he's up to?"

"I do, but in my own time and way. Come on. Let's get home. I have to get back in bed before Uncle realizes I'm gone."

We walked in silence for a while before he said, "I don't understand, Duncan. It looks to me like you went out of your way to follow Kikaku, then turned into...whatever...and beat the crap out of a Shimoshuki. Why wouldn't you want to pursue Kikaku immediately?"

"I just can't explain it right now." And I honestly couldn't. Shinji didn't know about what happened between me and Shi'tori, what I had done to her, or my reason to suspect Kikaku was a link to the Shimoshuki and the sudden interest they had in what we kept hidden and secret. Tonight's encounter had my suspicions trained on Shadow Kikaku. I sighed and felt my inner power finally subsided.

"Shinji, you were following Kikaku too, right?"

"Well, I was following who I *thought* was Kikaku. I didn't actually see him leave his house, but I was following a shadow that was close to the wooded area near his house. So, I assumed," Shinji said.

Great. That just blew my theory right out of the water. Shinji wasn't sure who he was following either and we couldn't assume, we had to be certain. It was a rule the Black Dragons lived by and one we had to instill in our minds.

We hurried home through the darkness, concealing ourselves and keeping low, and as we went I explained my new power to Shinji and insisted he keep it a secret. This was starting to get out of hand. One by one my friends were finding out about my odd power and I knew it would only be a matter of time before the entire village knew. All Shinobi of the Chiao had inner power, elemental energy and a special animal fighting style. The power we called forth was Ki based, and was nothing like mine. This odd voice and the power that accompanied it became more frightening the easier it came to bring forth, yet harder to make go away. Captain Yoshida may carry out his threat on me if I don't keep it under control. But how? It was a growing concern I had yet to unravel.

9

Subtle Warnings

It was almost three o'clock in the morning when I emerged from the closet and replaced the floorboards that concealed the secret passage in my room. I had weapons training at five o'clock and was completely wiped out. I wanted to lie down and sleep for a short while, to regain my strength and fight the fatigue in my brain. Instead, I sat on the edge of my bed and looked at myself in the mirror.

"What the..."

I stood and gazed at my reflection. Remnants of blood smeared my upper lip; as if I actually had a broken nose earlier it was now healed. I lifted my T-shirt and touched my ribs. To my amazement they weren't sore, didn't even hurt, and I could now breath deeply without wincing in pain. I sat back down on my bed and thought about this. That voice, and the blue flame power, it must heal. Weeks ago when I was fighting Shi'tori and her poison was coursing through my veins, I had allowed the inner power to take control of me because I was dying and unable to defend myself, or Mayumi. After Shi'tori was dead and I was able to regain a normal state, I had felt perfectly fine. I had never really thought about it before, but the poison had been purged from my system. When I fought the Shimoshuki tonight he punched me in the face and most likely broke my nose. I already had a cracked rib from the ordeal with the mountain trolls. Then I let the inner power take over tonight and now I was healed again.

"So, you heal me?" I said, hoping the blue flame thing heard me.

I listened for an answer, a whisper in my head.

Nothing.

It was just as well. To have a conversation with a voice in my head would be creepy. Then there was the issue with Kikaku or, better yet, the shadow figure of who I *thought* was Kikaku. He wasn't in his bed tonight, so he had to be somewhere. I saw a shadow in the forest and followed it. Shinji said he followed a shadow too - only it wasn't the same one I had followed. It was different, going in a separate direction. Did Shinji follow the real Kikaku and he gave him the slip? Did he follow the Shimoshuki? Or did I follow Kikaku?

I pinched between my eyes and released a sigh. This was making my head hurt. There were too many possibilities and without knowing the absolute truth I ran the risk of accusing Kikaku when I could be wrong. What if it was someone else? To accuse a pre-Black Dragon was taking a step into quick sand. The idea made my stomach hurt. A wrongful accusation would make me look bad in front of the elders, my uncle, Captain Yoshida and the other Black Dragon Squad members. I would get labeled before I even got into the squad.

Then there was the issue of why *I* was out running around late at night trying to track a fellow Shinobi. They could blame me instead of Kikaku and say I was setting him up to divert suspicion away from myself. To save my ass I would have to admit my suspicions, which could, once again, have implications for me if I were wrong.

And what of the Shimoshuki? He had given five hundred dollars to the shadow traitor for a piece of paper. What was on that paper, and who was this Lord Zahn he had mentioned? Whoever it was he wanted information about an item the Chiao Village kept hidden and secret and felt it would help in his world conquest. This foreign threat was exploiting help from our rival clan to get this special item and the Shimoshuki were willing to go to great lengths to get it for him. This, in itself, was worth telling the elders. If I did, however, I would have to explain myself and admit everything I knew...plus everything I had done – like killing Shi'tori.

No. I couldn't confide in anyone else just yet.

This wouldn't be easy, but I would have to find a way to get Kikaku to admit he was the traitorous teen. I sighed and paced around my room as I changed into clean clothes for weapons class. Time was getting close and I had to get moving no matter how tired I was. A ninja could function on very little sleep and I was at the top of my class.

In the back of my mind I felt a strong urge to confide in Uncle; to tell him everything. I knew he'd be discreet when he talked to the elders and would protect me from the secret wrath of Captain Yoshida. But what if his explanation raised too many questions, too many concerns against me? I'd be dead meat.

I decided against it for the moment and slid my swords out of the carry case, polished the blades to remove any remnants of blood and returned them to their rightful place on my back. I still had time, but decided to go early.

I stole to the front door. Someone sitting in the dim early morning light of the kitchen cleared his throat and I froze as I reached for the handle.

"And where were you tonight?"

It was Uncle and he didn't sound real happy with me.

"Uncle...well...I was..." I stumbled on my words, not sure what to say and I felt like a child caught red-handed. His stern gaze bore right through me and I succumbed. My head drooped in defeat. "I have no excuse, Uncle," I finally said in a small quiet voice.

"Is that so?" He leaned back in the chair and stroked his short graying beard. I could feel tension radiating from him and chose my next words carefully.

"With all due respect, Uncle, I'm going to weapons class now. Can we talk about this later?"

His eyes narrowed and in two steps he was upon me. His powerful grip on my arm reminded me he was only old in age, not in body and spirit. Sometimes he actually terrified me, but mostly he amazed me. Right now I felt a mixture of both.

"I think we can talk about it now," he said, leaning in close to my face.

He was pissed.

I was doomed.

"Uncle...look, it's like this..."

"Where did you go tonight, Duncan?"

"Out. Just out. That's all..."

"What were you doing?" he started to raise his voice with every question.

""Um, that's ...

"You better not be meeting with any boys and doing drugs!"

"What! No! No, Uncle, please, it's not like that. You wouldn't believe me if I told you."

He grabbed me by my neck, squeezed and slammed me against the wall close to the door. I desperately wanted to turn into a shadow and slide under the door just to get away from him, but I held firm and gave in. I had no other choice.

"Try me," he said, through clenched teeth.

For the next twenty minutes I relayed all that occurred that night, but broke it down because I didn't want to be late for class. Master Katsumi wasn't very forgiving. I had to explain my suspicions of Kikaku and why I felt the need to follow him. Uncle didn't interrupt and stroked his short beard while I talked faster than Mayumi's best friend, Lilly.

"So, you see, Uncle, I just wanted to find out for myself. To see if Kikaku was actually sneaking around late at night like the other kids were saying. I needed to know if he was a traitor, selling us out and why.

"And did you find the answers you seek?" Uncle finally stood from his comfortable spot at the kitchen table.

I sighed, face flushed with embarrassment. "No," I finally admitted.

"I think you're so upset with Kikaku constantly picking at you and trying to capture Mayumi's attention that you'd be willing to risk even your own reputation as a Shinobi to prove he's doing something unethical."

I hated to admit it, but he was right. Kikaku's relentless badgering of my fighting skills, the way he always made fun of me and how he flirted with Mayumi right in front of me every chance he got fueled my anger. But that wasn't all of it, there had to be more, and I knew there was an underlying suspicion deep in my gut, something else about Kikaku – I just didn't know what it was yet.

"Uncle, you're right about those things, but I feel, deep inside, there's something about Kikaku, something...well, not quite right," I said.

Uncle sighed and walked me over to the door; a silent signal our conversation was over.

"You may be right. He's become a powerful Shinobi and not always a team player. Kikaku has...history. As do all of our Shinobi. That's what makes each of us special, bringing unique fighting skills to our village," he said in a proud tone.

He opened the door and shooed me out. "Duncan, I'm going to say this once again, be careful with those you confront. I know you may believe Kikaku has a link with the Shimoshuki because of the kinoichi from several weeks ago, but that doesn't mean he's turned on the Chiao Clan, or that he's a traitor. There could be something else going on."

"Yes, sir," was all I said. And in my mind I thought, *and I'm going to find out what it is.*

I got to the weapons training area just in time. Class was about to start and though Master Katusmi eyed me annoyingly as I ran up, dropped my books and took my place next to Hikaru he didn't comment. I was glad, too.

"Where you been?" Hikaru said quietly out of the corner of his mouth.

"Got a lecture from Uncle first thing this morning," I said quietly.

"Duncan! Hikaru! Drop and give me twenty!" Master Katsumi bellowed.

We quickly did as he ordered, without protest, and without question. Talking in ranks was prohibited and something that had to be drilled into our heads early in training. I heard Mayumi and Yuji giggle, but nothing came from Akira. Perhaps he really had changed his attitude toward me.

"Okay, here's what were going to do today..." Master Katsumi paced back and forth, barking orders and explaining the morning exercise until we were finished pushups.

We spent the rest of our time training to defend from two attackers at once. I fought Akira and Hikaru first, using both swords and staying more on guard than actually fighting back. My teammates kept me trapped between them perfectly, like wolves circling prey, never letting up, never allowing an inch of retreat. I was impressed with how well they used eye and facial movements to project their ideas to each other, the silent communication our Shinobi used. The technique was unique to us, yet it was something that all ninja incorporated in some type of way.

Each of us took turns being in the middle. Mayumi surprised us most of all, using a circular sweeping technique with her fans and backhand springs in unison to duck, dodge and defend. When class was over two hours later I was thoroughly exhausted and more than happy to head to my next class.

With Mayumi on my arm and books hugged to my hip, the worries and confrontations of the past evening hours were but fleeting moments, strands of time deep in the shadows of my mind. No longer were the concerns of Kikaku, a shadow traitor, or the distant threat of the Shimoshuki and their unseen advisor plaguing my life. I was a teen again, with his girlfriend and going to class, yet living in the modern world under strict life rules as an assassin in training, a protector, and a hired hand. It wasn't until I passed Morgan sitting balanced on a fence that I was pulled back to the reality of my growing problems.

"Hey, Duncan," Morgan said in an almost bored tone that forced me to halt.

I turned toward Morgan, but didn't answer right away; I was suddenly too intrigued at how he was lounging on such a thin surface. It seemed physically impossible, but Morgan was a strange one and I simply accepted that because he was Morgan he could do these odd things and it was okay. Mayumi looked at him quizzically and cocked her head. Even after saying hello, Morgan seemed to not notice us. He simply turned a page in the book he was reading, *Helter Skelter Analogies,* and sighed deeply. I got the feeling he wanted to tell me something.

"What's up?" I finally said, stepping closer to him.

"Oh, not much. Life as we know it is coming to an end." He breathed a deep, troubled tone that made me feel we were all doomed.

"Oh, um, that's cool. Time will tell, huh?"

"Guess so," he sighed again, shrugged and turned a page. "Learn any new attack moves lately?"

I stiffened and cleared my throat, and then pulled Mayumi close and kissed her on the cheek.

"You go on ahead. I'll catch up," I said.

"Okay. Don't be too long. Bye, Morgan," Mayumi waved as she walked away to class.

Seconds passed as I watched her. My head tilted to the side and my mouth hung open slightly. I shook myself and realized I was staring at her gently swaying hips and the way her long pony-tail swished with her body movements. It was a work of art. When I turned back to Morgan I saw he was doing the same thing. I stepped even closer to him.

"You obviously know something you'd like to share," I said loud enough to startle the skinny, pale infiltrator.

Morgan put a bookmark at his page and hopped down off the fence. He was a bit shorter than me with less body mass, bad posture and deep-set eyes. He adjusted his long bangs in his face to hide those eyes and leaned close.

"You need to be careful. The Shimoshuki are advanced fighters – but not very smart."

"I'm finding that out," I admitted.

"Look. All I'm saying is that they teach their young Shinobi how to connect with their inner animal, their *aggressive* inner animal, entirely too early in their training." He paused and looked around to make sure no one was listening before continuing. "This fighting style gives them tremendous power, and they thirst for more each time they use it, becoming more aggressive. That's the curse of learning the technique too early as a Shinobi. When we, the Chiao, tap into ours, it's with a clear mind and set purpose. They do it to bully, control and destroy."

"Not a good combination," I mused.

"They've also been in contact with Master Tsubasa."

"Master Tsubasa. Who's he?"

"Only a legendary assassin," Morgan said, as if I should've known. "He's ruthless, cunning...the best ever, but now rogue. He always gets his target. Rumor's are that he's dead, but he's not. Used to be part of the Tesenga Clan that's now long gone."

"What's that got to do with me?" I'd learned that Morgan didn't tell you anything unless there was a purpose.

"Just thought you'd like to know."

"That's not an answer," I scowled. He quickly changed the subject.

"You're aware of the nightly excursions made by several teen Shinobi in our village?"

"Several?" I was shocked that Kikaku wasn't the only one. "How many? Who are they? What's going on?"

"That, my friend, is a very good question," he started to walk away, and then paused. "Watch who you trust. Even your closest friend could turn on you."

The initial shock of his statement made me hesitate for only a moment. "What? Morgan, wait!"

It was too late. He may have looked skinny and weak, but Morgan was fast with his flash step and moved through the crowd of teens going to class before I got another word out.

10

Read Between the Lines

My mind was in a fog the rest of the day. Fatigue, my conversation with Morgan and the reasons behind the fight with the Shimoshuki swam in my head. I was so preoccupied with my thoughts that I hardly participated in any classes or talked to my friends. Mayumi was the only real comfort in my day and she silently, yet lovingly, kept a watchful eye on me. If she thought I didn't notice she was mistaken, for it was a special trait all the females in our village had. I was just a bit surprised she had developed it so early. As I walked her home from classes I felt even more of a bond between us.

"Lilly is having an ice cream social at her house after dinner. We should go," she said, then continued to chatter endlessly about cooking and the upcoming festival in the city. The more she talked the less I listened, but I smiled and nodded as I've seen Makoto and Kenji do with their girls. The more she thought I was listening the more she hugged my arm and laid her head on my shoulder. The smell of flowers from her hair drifted to my nose and I sighed with satisfaction.

I wanted to kiss her – a real kiss, not that cheek stuff. I didn't think she would mind, but I also didn't want her to feel I was moving too fast. I didn't want to upset her and force her from my side. To me it was important to be careful with Mayumi. She was so special and the last thing I wanted was to mess everything up before I had to chance to explore our deepest feelings.

"Okay," I finally said, interrupting her chattering.

"Okay what?" she looked puzzled and I instantly felt a screw up just happened. I missed part of what she was saying.

"Um, okay, let's go to Lilly's house for ice cream." It was the only save I could come up with.

"Duncan, you're so wonderful," she cooed.

We were almost at her house and I felt the moment was right. I stopped and turned to face her. Her eyes were like pools of liquid onyx as she gazed into my face. She was so beautiful. My heart raced, my mouth went dry and I paused to brush her cheek with the back of my fingers then traced one finger down her jaw line to her perfect lips.

This was it. I knew she wanted me to kiss her. She'd been waiting for this moment and I was going to take the plunge. She stepped closer - pressed herself against me. Our foreheads touched, then our noses, I could hear her breath quicken in anticipation and it drove me on. I slowly dipped my face down, our lips barely touched - then we heard an earth-shattering shout from her front door.

"Mayumi! Time to come in!" It was her mother, saving her little girl.

Mrs. Tanaka was a sweet lady, but her voice shot right though me like a buzz saw and the interruption made Mayumi jump and back away, blushing beautifully and tugging at her long ponytail in embarrassment.

"I, um, guess I better go," she shied away and tried to laugh. "I'll see you at Lilly's later on. Okay?"

"Sure." I watched until she was safely inside. Mrs. Tanaka

gave me a scowl, but right before she turned away I saw a slight smile pass over her lips.

Disappointed, I trudged away and headed home. "Damn it! I was this close!" I said to myself.

The only good thing that came of the interruption was that I now knew Mayumi was ready for our first kiss and I couldn't wait for another perfect opportunity. Next time we wouldn't be anywhere near her mother.

My musings were interrupted as I approached the gazebo next to a stream. Surrounded by weeping cherry trees it was one of my favorite spots; a special place where my sister, Ruby, or Jewel, as Uncle called her, and I would sit and talk about stuff. Currently it was marred by the presence of Kenji, Makoto and Kikaku. Their conversation quieted the closer I got. They watched me with interest. I tried to ignore them, as always.

"Ready for another visit to the Old Mill?" Makoto said with a laugh.

I threw him a hard look and kept walking.

"He's not that tough," Kenji said to Makoto. "I don't think he even made it up there."

"He was probably too frightened and ran away," Kikaku laughed.

"How would you know Kikaku? Not everyone runs around late at night in secret like you do!" I shot back, but instantly regretted it.

The remark wiped the smile right off Kikaku's face and in a matter of strides he quickly caught up with me and stepped in my path.

"Just what are you implying?" he towered over me by a few inches, but I wasn't afraid and met his verbal challenge with a steely gaze.

"Take it how you want, jerk!"

"Ooooo," Kenji and Makoto chorused.

"Well, well, well," Makoto said stepping forward. "Looks like he wants to accuse a pre-Black Dragon."

"Dragons don't bully. Why don't you practice some of what you've learned?" I clenched my fists.

"I think he wants to get his ass kicked," Kenji muttered from a few steps away.

"Once again, Dragons don't bully," I said never taking my eyes from Kikaku's.

"Maybe I'm not the one running around late at night? Maybe you've been starting rumors just to get everyone suspicious of me?" Kikaku growled in my face.

"Figures you'd say something as lame as that," I said in a low tone. "Anything to keep attention away from what you're really all about." It was direct and to the point and not how I wanted to initially handle the interrogation. In fact, I wasn't even discrete like I had planned and it earned me a punch to the gut. Kikaku may be strong, but I had a highly developed body and doubled over only slightly as air rushed out of my lungs. He then snatched me up by the front of my T-shirt and jerked me forward. A breeze instantly kicked up around my feet, wisps of my hair lifted up as if they were alive and I could feel a darkening in my eyes. I tried to keep my head down so he wouldn't see.

"Shut your mouth, idiot! It's just rumors! Don't you ever repeat that stuff – ever!" he shouted only inches from my face.

I had had enough. I raised my head and stared back at him, rage coursing through my body.

"See! Do you see?" Makoto stuttered, pointed and backed away.

"Duncan...your eyes," Kenji said in disbelief.

I couldn't stop it, I just kept getting madder and I felt an unease rise like bile in my throat. It stuck there and hovered, almost like the feeling had a mind of its own, contemplating, considering. This was something I never experienced before and I wanted to act fast before it got out of hand. I had to get away from Kikaku and calm down, to regain myself and get control.

I lashed out with a front snap kick to the chest, forcing Kikaku to release his hold on me. He stumbled backwards, hand on his chest, heaving to catch his breath. The force of my kick projected me backwards as well. I landed a few feet away, dropped my books and drew both swords without hesitation.

"Bring it!" I challenged.

Kikaku drew his katana. The metallic *zing* of his blade leaving the scabbard echoed as the air became very still. We held our positions, each waiting for the other to advance. My breathing labored as I tried to calm down. I wanted to regain myself, but a pull from within begged me to finish him.

Do it...

That voice again.

You need me...

It preyed on my deepest fear and I started to doubt if I had the skills to beat Kikaku. He was a pre-Black Dragon after all, older than me with more training under his belt. Still, I thought I could take him. With the help of this inner power I could beat him to a pulp. Yeah, maybe I did need it?

Yes...

But wait! No! I couldn't do that to a fellow Shinobi, no matter how much I hated him. Then again...

"What's going on here?" a loud stern voice cut through the silence like a bladed chain whip and it made us freeze in our tracks. "Well? I'm waiting for an answer!"

It was Yamamoto sensei. He stood not far from us, scowling, with one hand on his cane; the other held art supplies and brushes.

"Put away your weapons and come before me at once!"

We rushed to do as commanded and fell on one knee before the old ninja, looking like relaxed runners at the starting line.

"Nowhere is it written – ever! – ever! that Shinobi from the Chiao turn on each other. Never! I don't care what your differences are, this is not acceptable."

I felt myself flinch every time he emphasized the words 'ever' and 'never' and out of the corner of my eye saw Kikaku do the same. The interruption was good for me; it allowed me to gain control.

"I'm very disappointed in both of you. Kikaku, you, above all, know better. I'll have to report this to Captain Yoshida."

"Yes, sir," Kikaku's voice was tight and angry and it sounded like he was trying to hold back from wanting to leap at Yamamoto sensei's face and maul him. "And Duncan, I know you were only trying to defend yourself, but you should never draw your weapons against a fellow Shinobi. You've been warned about this behavior in the past."

"Yes, sir," I said quickly, already regretting how I acted.

"On your feet!" Yamamoto sensei snapped.

We did as commanded. In an act of self-redemption I turned toward Kikaku and said," I'm sorry for what I said and how I said it..."

"Well, it's good to see your learning your place..." Kikaku started in a cocky manner, but I quickly cut him off.

"But I meant what I implied," I paused and glared at him. "I just should've handled it a different way."

Tension mounted. We held each other's gaze a moment longer. Yamamoto sensei interrupted with a sharp slap to our calves with his cane.

"You're both dismissed, but this is my first, and last, warning. Don't let this ever happen again!"

"Yes, sir!" We bowed respectfully as Yamamoto sensei hobbled away.

I turned on my heel, grabbed my books and quickly walked away. I wanted to gain a good distance from Kikaku before something else happened. We were lucky this time. Next time I could be kicked out of training and forced to be a cook for the rest of my life. I wasn't about to give Kikaku that satisfaction.

* * *

With the confrontation behind me I looked forward to a more enjoyable evening. As promised, I went over to Lilly's house to meet Mayumi after dinner. Lots of kids our age were there, even Kenji and Makoto. Lilly held onto Kenji's bulging biceps and Makoto was wooing the latest choice from his entourage of young women hoping to capture his heart. As for me, well, all I needed sat close to my side, enjoying ice cream and allowing me to wrap an arm around her and snuggle.

Once again, the worries and troubles of a pending turmoil, with me in the middle, were far away – until I spotted Morgan not far from where I sat. Just his presence sent a slight jolt of warning though me.

As always Morgan was reading a book of some strange origin, not really paying attention to people around him while eating ice cream. His eyes met mine from over top his book and quickly flickered to the approaching form of Hikaru. I was happy to see my best friend, but he didn't look real happy to see me. In fact, he looked run down and exhausted. I waved him over to sit with me and Mayumi and as he pushed, struggled and finally emerged from a crowd of teens he had three beautiful young girls clinging to his arms. They swooned and cooed and stroked his overly long hair.

"Oh, Hikaru, let me comb it for you."

"I saw you in taijutsu class, you're amazing."

"Let me practice massage on you, Hikaru."

Mayumi scrunched up her nose in disdain at all the fussing from the girls then grabbed my arm, batted her long lashes and silently mocked them. It made me laugh and Hikaru noticed us acting out.

"Sorry, ladies, I'll catch up with you later, okay?" Hikaru tried to let them down easy and the three girls let out a disappointed "Awwwww," before reluctantly turning away.

"S'up dude?" he said and plopped down next to me.

"You look wiped out," I said.

"I am. Sooo tired." He yawned and stretched.

"Why? It's only seven o'clock. The night's still young," I said. My trained eye scoped him out, seeking for a reason. This wasn't like him at all. Something had changed.

"You act like you've been up all night and most of the day," Mayumi said with a little giggle.

Though I knew she didn't mean anything by it, her comment struck a nerve. My eyes shifted over to where Morgan still stood reading his book. His watchful gaze met mine right before he snapped his book shut and walked away. The action was almost as if he said something final and I searched my memory for the meaning. Then it came to me, and the words he said only hours ago drifted to mind. Suddenly I realized what Morgan was implying when he said I should be careful who I trust, that even my closest friend could turn on me. Was he talking about Hikaru? Morgan also said *several* teens have been sneaking out late at night and Mayumi's innocent comment also made me realize that maybe, possibly, Hikaru could be one of them. But why? For what reason?

"Me? Out all night?" Hikaru gave a nervous, unconvincing

laugh and said, "Yeah, I know. What can I say? The ladies keep me busy."

I didn't believe for a minute that Hikaru was staying up late at night to woo a girl. Or even to woo several girls. His father would hit the roof if he knew his only son was sneaking out at night and not getting his rest to bring their family honor every day he was in training. So, that led me to the dreaded question – was Hikaru one of the 'several' running around late at night?

My suspicions now shifted and a chill ran up my spine. What if Hikaru was the one I saw with the Shimoshuki last night and not Kikaku? What if my best friend was the rogue teen ninja selling out his clan for information? And if he was, what was I, his best friend since grade school, supposed to do about it? The inner duties that had been ingrained in us since the age of five ruled my heart and insisted that I report him, but my love for him as a brother and close friend fought with it. Besides, on what grounds would I report him? I couldn't report him any more than I could Kikaku. I was stuck. My suspicions split. Now I'd have to follow Hikaru and Kikaku to find out what was really going on.

After the quick musing, I let out an equally phony laugh, clapped Hikaru on the shoulder and said, "Yeah, you look like you have your hands full."

"Well, you know, it's tough to be me," Hikaru laughed again and went to stand, staggered and quickly regained himself.

Was he high?

"You all right, Hikaru?" Mayumi said.

"Oh, sure, I just lost my balance. That's all. I'm not gonna stay. I need to go home." He bumbled through his words, gestured with his thumb towards home and slowly backed away.

"Okay, I'll see you for weapons training in the morning," I said, waving as he trotted off.

Seconds ticked by as I stared at his retreating form.

"Mayumi..." I started, but was quickly cut off.

"I'm all over it. Let's go," she said, standing and discarding what was left of her ice cream cone.

"Hold up. I don't think you should come with me. It might look suspicious."

She narrowed her eyes and fixed me with a hard stare, challenging me with that silent communication. It wasn't that I didn't want her to come. It was more I was afraid two would be noticed more than one and, besides, she might get hurt. I knew she could take care of herself, but she was my girl and I wanted to protect her.

"Mayumi, please, I want to follow him. Alone. If he sees both of us the reason will be too obvious. I stand a better chance," I explained, trying to take her hands in mine.

She quickly put them behind her back and wouldn't let me touch her.

"You have to admit it makes sense." I paused and looked over my shoulder. Hikaru was nearly out of sight. "Baby, please."

That got her. She was completely taken by surprise when I called her 'Baby' and her icy demeanor instantly thawed. She stared at me blankly for a moment and I took the opportunity to gently grip her upper arms, pull her close and tease her with the promise of a kiss. Mayumi sucked in her breath at the gesture and had nothing more to say when I released her and turned to run after Hikaru.

I trailed entirely too far behind my best friend and took a position at the side of his house after he went inside. All was quiet, no shouting from parents or ruckus from siblings, which was odd. When the light came on in his room I ducked down low, yet still watched from a nearby tree. Hikaru flopped in bed and turned out the light. I was disappointed; yet skeptical that there still may be an underlying reason for Hikaru's unusual behavior. I hated to have to do it, but I needed to spy on my best friend. I whipped out a kuni, spun it around one finger, allowed it to settle perfectly in the palm of my hand and gouged the blade into the tree. I then plucked a single blade of grass while waiting for sap to ooze out of the cut. Once I had enough, I touched each end of the of grass blade to the sap. Stealthily I approached Hikaru's closed bedroom window and attached each end of the grass to the sill and the pane. I couldn't hang around for too long, Uncle would want to know where I am. But once Uncle fell asleep I could sneak out. If the grass was broken I'll know that Hikaru had snuck out. Tracking him would be more difficult even for a highly trained Shinobi, but at least I'd know he was actually running around at night. Trying to figure out what he was up to would be the other problem.

11

Precursor

It was well past midnight when I made it to Hikaru's window.
Just as suspected, the blade of grass was broken. My heart sank
at the thought of my best friend corrupted and rogue, selling out
his clan to the Shimoshuki. It also reminded me that I still
needed to locate the item of interest, the one the Shimoshuki
wanted so badly, the one they wanted to sell to a man named
Zahn who would use it for his own personal reasons. Whatever
this item was, it must be powerful, or wonderful, or both. Uncle
wasn't going to tell me. I was ambushed once by a Black Dragon
trying to follow him, thinking he would lead me to it. There had
to be another way to find out.

My mind reeled with the possibilities as I found Hikaru's
footprints not far from his house. I melted into the night shadows and silently moved through the forest. Hopefully he didn't
have much of a head start, and unfortunately I had no way of
knowing when he left. The footprints disappeared after a few
yards. He must've taken to the trees, or the forest floor vegeta-
tion was just so incredibly thick it blocked my view. My guess was

Hikaru took to the trees and I did the same. The branch shook only slightly as it took my weight and from that point on I traveled silently through the thick trees. I wasn't sure which direction to go, so I trusted my instinct to choose the way for me. As if guided by an inner beacon I headed off to my right like I was going toward the city and highway. Why? I didn't know. It just felt right. The air felt heavy with warmth and humidity and it made my T-shirt cling to my skin. It was going to be a hot summer. I moved swiftly, disturbing the active night creatures and allowing any rustling I caused to blend with their movements. I traveled this way for a good fifteen minutes until the clanging of blades caught my attention.

Off to the right and deeper into the forest were the sounds of battle. My heart pounded with excitement. Could this be Hikaru? Maybe I was wrong about him? Maybe he was only out every night doing what I was doing – trying to track down a thief, a traitor, or someone he suspected? The sounds became louder the closer I got and I zeroed in on the fighters within moments.

Amidst a cropping of pines offset by a small forest of giant bamboo were two figures engaged in a heated battle. Both wore black, their faces concealed except their eyes. One opponent was tall and thickly built, while the other was a few inches shorter and had the body mass of a young man. The smaller ninja welded a katana and the other used a double-bladed spear, a bo staff with a curved double blade at each end. It was rare to see such a weapon; they weren't made much anymore and the art of usage died along with their masters a century ago. This ninja spun and slashed with his spear like it was child's play, spinning it around his hands and arms, then catching it and extending the weapon toward his opponent, nearly impaling him. They kept up the violent dance, each fully intent on killing the other, only to strike and push away. At first I was mesmerized by their skill, but after a short while it started to become pointless. Either they were evenly matched and this fight was going nowhere, or the bigger guy was only playing with the smaller one.

With frustration setting in, the smaller guy suddenly charged while shouting and slashing his katana in a crazy spiral motion. The bigger guy retreated to the bamboo, spun his spear and sliced them at an angle, leaving short, sharp, pointed ends sticking up in its wake. I instantly saw his intention. The smaller man understood as well and jumped up onto a low tree branch right across from me, then came at his opponent from a different direction. The battle continued as the larger man moved to what he felt was a more agreeable distance, stuck his spear in the ground and moved his hands in a most peculiar way. Circling his arms in a large counterclockwise motion, he then brought his hands together, one resting over the other and shaped them like he was holding a ball. The air instantly went still and heavy, like all the wind was being sucked out of the area. I put a hand to my throat trying to breathe. The smaller man did the same. A blast of wind was suddenly released, which sent the smaller man toppling backwards, end over end, and slammed him into the base of the very tree I was hiding in. The jolt of the impact shook me from my secure hiding spot and sent me to the ground. The battle abruptly ended with my appearance.

I was just as surprised as they were; this type of thing never happened to me.

"Who the hell are you?" the smaller man said. His voice was muffled through his mask; he didn't quite sound like Hikaru and his hair was tucked down into his gi - but his eyes....

I quickly struggled to my feet and faced them. "I think a better question is who are you two?"

Tension mounted as they sized me up. I knew the look and the subtle body movements of an impending attack. I was ready.

The smaller man came at me with mounted fury, running full force. With minimal effort, I stepped slightly to the side, placed my leg behind his, and grabbed his face with my hand. His feet shot out from under him as I took control and slammed him to the ground in one fluent motion. My new move. I was beginning to really like it and I grinned mischievously as he laid still, moaning and complaining about his back.

The large man took up his double-bladed spear and slowly sidestepped in a circle, never taking his eyes off me, every muscle in his body noticeably ready for an attack.

"I'll ask again. Who are you two? Why are you out here?" I demanded, slowly moving with my opponent, waiting for him to attack first.

"Why should we answer to you?"

He was American, which raised another question, though it shouldn't matter; there were lots of Americans living in Japan. But why was an American ninja fighting with this other guy in the woods, late at night?

"I am a ninja of the Chiao Village. This is our land and we're to check out any suspicious activity." Okay, so that was stretching the truth just a bit, and I wasn't a Black Dragon or security, but I felt I made an impression by the way his eyes widened ever so slightly.

He started spinning his spear in a windmill fashion. I sank into my knees, stayed low, and waited. It was quite obvious he wasn't going to give me an answer to my questions.

Without warning, the smaller man jumped up from the ground and took off through the forest. The distraction caught me off guard and my first instinct was to go after him, but my opponent seized the opportunity and was on me with the fastest flash step I'd ever seen. He caught me across the chest with his forearm and slammed my back into a tree. Air rushed out of my lungs for only an instant, but it was an instant too long. Before I knew it the point of his spear blade was poised under my chin. To move a muscle would've been fatal.

"Hmmm, you look vaguely familiar," he breathed, leaning in close to my face. He then sucked in his breath and his eyes widened. "Kato?"

I stared at him, held his gaze, a fleeting moment passed where I couldn't speak. Then I scowled and said, "How do you know my father?"

He released his hold on me, stepped back and threw a smoke pellet between us. The air was thick with smoke and I coughed and tried to wave it away, but knew he was gone. Who was he? Who was the other guy? Why were they out here? And why did he call me by my father's name? They were questions I would never get answered at this rate.

I wiped a hand over my face, blew out frustration and paused to listen to the night. All was quiet. The night creatures had resumed their activities in the area now that the fighting was over. I wanted to go after those two, but knew it would be a waste of time. They must be far away by now.

I scuffed the toe of my tabi boot on the ground, and then turned to go home. Just as I did a shadow moved next to a tree. I squinted at it and looked deeper into the night. Nothing was there - yet something was. Suddenly it was as if the night shadows took on a life of their own, shaping and molding into a form that wasn't quite discernible at first. I stepped back, putting some distance between myself and the shadow next to the tree.

The shadow moved ever so slightly and an alarm went off in my head. I pulled both dragon swords. The blades glinted in the moonlight as I positioned them to defend. The shadow inched away from the tree, becoming an entity of its own, growing into the shape of a human, with one arm exposed and a very large wrapped item strapped to its back. It could be a weapon of some sort, though, if so, it was entirely too big. Stark white, unkempt hair spilled over a plain black headband. The ninja face guard was intricately carved metal in the shape of a fierce spirit scowl attached to black cloth that tied around the stranger's head. He was tall, and his eyes told that he was older than Master Katsumi, but just as thickly built. He stared at me with arms folded, not moving, not speaking and not making any intentional movements.

"What do you want?" I said gruffly.

He didn't speak.

I was very uneasy about this. It was like he was sizing me up; trying to figure me out and I had no clue who he was or why I was an object of curiosity. Either way, it was clear I was his target.

Mounting fear threatened to take hold and my heart pounded hard against my chest. Should I engage this guy? I could easily call on my inner voice and summon the special power growing inside me for any help with fighting him, but something told me not to. For a ninja, it wasn't always about stealth and fighting. It was also about running away and hiding, waiting for an opportune moment to strike; maybe not this day, but someday you would eventually get your target. Master Jun harped on the fact that it was always about timing and patience. At the moment, running didn't seem like such a bad idea. Besides, I had no idea who this guy was, or what he wanted, let alone what kind of a skilled fighter I was up against. After all, he did manipulate the shadows, hiding within them and unveiling himself when he felt the time was right. It was time I did the same.

With my best sleight-of-hand I pulled out a smoke pellet and threw it between us. The smoke thickened, quickly enveloping me in a hazy blanket. Now was my chance. Instead of jumping into the trees, I melted with the shadows of the earth and ran, quickly putting distance between us. I was instantly panicked. Every sound around me - a snap, a rustle - signaled I was being followed. I could feel his presence close by; his very essence clung to my back, slowed me down, and dragged me backwards. Was it the night shadows coming to life and grabbing at me? Was he a Shadow Master? I had to get away from this guy.

My heart raced as I dodged the sounds. I forced my body to go faster as I zipped around trees, shrubs and croppings of boulders, but he stayed with me, matching my every step, my every move. This was insane!

"I need help, please, help..." I muttered under my breath, calling forth the energy deep inside my soul.

It didn't answer. What was I to do? I knew I couldn't take this guy on my own, no matter how advanced I was. He was skilled. Scary skilled. And probably knew things I hadn't learned yet.

Come on...do this for me or I might die... I thought in my head as I jumped over a fallen tree. The sound of metal being unsheathed vibrated in my ears. My imagination went wild and I suspected he was taking out that large weapon on his back.

Then I want to stay...

"No!" I shouted, cutting hard to the right and barely missing a tree. A kuni stuck in the tree, just as I ran past.

I knew it. Whatever this energy source was inside me it had a mind of its own. Each time it surfaced it took longer to make go away. Now it wanted to stay at the surface, most likely to control me.

I didn't have time to argue with this thing; the smell of cold steel was close. Sensing my enemy's presence, I jumped and spun in the air while slashing with my twin dragon swords. The blades met with his forearm, encased in a black bracer covered in long curved blades. I'd never seen anything like it before. The Shadow Master let out a little laugh; quite pleased at my surprise and used the pause to his advantage. With a scratching *zing!* he ripped his bracer free of my blades, circled his arm around and came at me with a back strike. I blocked again, and then we zipped from tree to tree to boulder, pushing off each, twisting in the air and executing strikes and blocks so fast I almost couldn't keep up. Sooner or later this guy was going to take a chunk out of me with his bladed bracer.

Come on voice, if I die so do you. I thought urgently.

Warmth ignited in my center and a surge of painful energy coursed through my veins, heating me up, causing my breath to quicken, my head to pound, and then suddenly my enhanced eyesight and hearing kicked in...and something else. Speed. It was the same thing I had felt the day Hikaru and I were attacked by the three Shimoshuki teens. On that day I had power that allowed me to run faster than ever and now I had it once more.

The Shadow Master's movements suddenly seemed very slow and I picked up the sound of a kuni being pulled from his knee-high boot. I chanced a look over my shoulder. He was upon me, one hand reaching for my throat, the other drawing back for the kill. In sudden desperation I turned and kicked him in the chest with all the force I could muster, threw two smoke pellets between us and took to the trees. In the blink of an eye I lost track of time and my enemy.

Within moments I was at the edge of the forest, a huge span of distance now between us. I paused and listened. No sound of pursuit. The night creatures were not disturbed by my presence or from any one else. I squatted down, blending with the earth, and watched the forest for several minutes.

Nothing.

Quiet.

I blew out a nervous breath and tried to relax. Finally it felt safe to duck into my secret entrance that would take me to my bedroom, but deep inside I was paranoid and prayed that I would never run into that guy again.

12

Secret Mission

The next day was like any other. Even though I was exhausted from my encounter with the Shadow Master, I was at weapons training at five in the morning. Hikaru was overly tired and grumpy and kept complaining that his back hurt. It raised suspicions in my mind. Perhaps he really was the guy I tried my new move on last night? If he was, why then was he out late at night fighting with an American ninja? I wanted to say something to him and it ate at my gut that I couldn't -or shouldn't. Part of being a good ninja was to keep information to yourself, wait until you have all the facts, and then confront your target. The Black Dragons did this all the time. It was part of the secrecy they had to uphold. Having such a high position within our village and constantly working with the government was a huge responsibility and required the utmost discretion in all that they did. I wanted to be just like them.

Though I kept this all in mind it didn't help with how I felt about Hikaru. What started out as suspicion against Kikaku, which still hadn't changed, now expanded to Hikaru. The thought of him turned traitor left a sour taste in my mouth and made my stomach twist. Unwillingly I kept an eye on him throughout the day; I looked for any signs he might give proving he was the guy from last night. It was easier to watch Hikaru; I had several classes with him. Kikaku was a different story. A pre-Black Dragon wasn't as easy to observe. However, he was involved with our Night Ops training twice a week and tonight was no exception.

Dressed in civilian clothes, we lined up in front of the fake buildings we used to destroy, tear up and burn down, only to have them rebuilt to do all over again. It was just normal training for a young teen assassin. A slight smile touched my lips as I remembered some of the crazy things I did in those buildings just to complete my 'mission.' The sound of approaching footsteps snapped me back to attention. Master Jun stood before us. Next to him were Kikaku, Makoto and Kenji dressed in civilian clothes, as well. They each held keys and a clipboard.

Many of the guys chatted excitedly amongst themselves about the three pre-Black Dragons assisting with our training again. I wasn't so impressed.

"What's all the fuss about?" Shinji suddenly appeared at my side, arms crossed and head cocked to the side. He wasn't real crazy about Kikaku, Makoto and Kenji either.

"I have no idea," I said with a shrug and roll of my eyes. The thought of those three being in charge made my head hurt. "Where's Masa?"

"At the end of the line." Shinji muttered then explained so that no one else would over hear. "I was trying to teach him to focus his Ki and channel it down his staff like I can do and it didn't work out very well. He burned his fingers."

I leaned back slightly and looked down the line of guys. Masa noticed me and waved. Band-aids were wrapped around each of his fingertips. I sort of felt sorry for Masa. He tried so hard and yet always fell short. It was his own fault, however - mentally he needed to be more grown-up.

"If he would just get serious and focus he could do it." Shinji sighed and placed his hands on his hips. "Duncan, I'm really starting to think he'll be left behind while the rest of us become Black Dragons, or guards, or whatever we all want to be and he'll just..."

"All right. Listen up," Master Jun's commanding voice instantly silenced us. "Tonight we're going to do something different from anything you've ever done before. Gather around." He motioned for us to come closer and sit on the ground. Once he had our attention he continued. "Up until now your training has been teaching you how to infiltrate the enemy's stronghold, sneak in, gain information and sneak out, and even getting in, getting caught yet still figuring out how to complete the mission. Everything is based on the completion of the mission - no matter what. Tonight you're going to get a chance to use some of those skills, but this will not be just an exercise. This will be the real thing." He paused and looked us over before continuing.

"It's been discovered that the Shimoshuki are undergoing secret meetings with outside forces." I raised an eyebrow, knowing full well where that information came from. "Now, we're not sure who their new allies are, but the Black Dragons are working on it. The Shimoshuki's interest in our village has grown. A few of their scouts have been caught sneaking around, looking for something..."

"Did we find out what it was they were looking for?" Shimo said. I knew he was concerned; his father was a guard at City Hall where the elders presided. It was the first place that would get attacked if an invasion were to take place.

Master Jun gave Shimo a very serious look and released a deep sigh. "They swallowed poison pills before we could interrogate them," he said as if it was something to be expected. "You're the best Night Ops training group I've had in years. Therefore, I've elected all of you to participate. Gentlemen, tonight you will accompany these three pre-Black Dragons on a mission."

Mumbled chatter immediately hummed throughout the group. When it didn't stop Makoto stepped forward and put up his hand. The guys immediately fell silent once more. Makoto then stepped back next to Kenji, arms folded across his strong chest. I'd never seen him in this state of mind before; bold and silent, yet powerful in his own right, commanding respect without strutting around. I was actually impressed and when he cast a glance my way I gave him a short upward nod and a small smile. He didn't acknowledge, but I know he noticed.

"You'll be broken up into groups. Each group with a Team Leader," Master Jun motioned to the pre-Black Dragons. "You will listen to your Team Leader and follow his orders. Your Team Leader will brief you on your mission."

I was paired up with Shimo, Daichi and Tai. Our Team Leader was Kenji. Shinji had Kakiku as his Team Leader and Masa was with Makoto. We each stocked ourselves with kuni, throwing stars, rope, and various other easily concealed weapons; tucking them into pants, belts, socks and even holsters worn on the back and under loose-fitting jackets. Our swords, sais and other large weapons were left for the night. Once we were set Kenji led us away from the training site and toward the main road that marks the entrance to the Chiao Village. The other teams followed. I was a bit disappointed I wasn't with Kikaku. It would've been a prime way to keep an eye on him. Since we were going to be observing the Shimoshuki, and Kikaku was most likely the traitor selling us out, my guess was that he would slip up tonight. It would be an opportune moment for him to sneak a conversation and I wanted to be there to catch him.

"All right, ladies, listen up," Kenji said, quite pleased that he was in charge. "This is what's going to happen so I'll break it down for you." We paused at the main road. Parked and waiting for us were three pickup trucks. Kenji stopped next to a black one. The other groups branched off to each of their trucks. "Each group has a slightly different objective. Yours will be to casually observe any Shimoshuki hanging out in town."

"Town?" Tai said.

"Yeah, we're going into Mizzaru. Not the city. Apparently intelligence has reported a meeting to take place tonight at a restaurant in town. That's where we'll be." Kenji spun the keys on his finger, skillfully caught them and unlocked the truck door. "One up front with me, three in the back. Let's move out!"

Moments later we were flying down the highway to Mizzaru, a local town only twenty minutes away from the Chiao Village. It wasn't a very large town, but still housed a ton of people. Uncle used to take me there a lot for ice cream, the movies, or to just shop around when I was younger. He still did, but our casual visits had become fewer and farther between now that my training had increased. Besides, I had my bike and could go alone if I wanted.

Mizzaru was beautifully laid out with temples, gardens, shops, housing and every inch was landscaped to perfection. My favorite part of Mizzaru was Crane Plaza, named for the lake close by where flocks of beautiful white cranes hung out. The plaza had every kind of shop you could imagine lining both sides of the busy streets. It was dotted with restaurants, and also included an outdoor skate park and play area. Down at the far end of the plaza were the dance clubs, which were the places my friends and I couldn't wait to check out when we got older.

Kenji drove into a high-rise parking garage, went to the fourth level and parked. I didn't see Makoto or Kikaku's trucks and wondered why.

"Kenji," I said, jumping out of the truck bed and approaching him. "Where are the others?"

"They chose different areas of the plaza to park so it wouldn't look suspicious to any Shimoshuki that might be observing the area." He pulled out his clipboard and started writing something down while looking around.

"One other thing," I said, leaning closer to him. He paused from writing and looked at me from over the clipboard. "Why use us? I'm not completely accepting what Master Jun said, that we're the best training group he's ever had. A few of us aren't up to par."

He gave me a hard stare and became very serious. "You guys really are the best he's had, but the truth is, Duncan, a group of kids are less suspicious. He had to get special permission from the elders to allow this mission. The Shimoshuki already know we take our kids here from time to time so they can have some fun and cut loose. So, this is no big deal."

The reasoning was flawless.

"Besides, this is a reality check. If the Shimoshuki attack us now, even at this stage of your training, you guys have to be ready." He threw the clipboard on the seat and shut the door, his face solemn. "No more fun and games. This is serious stuff." He turned away from me, a signal our personal conversation was over. "Alright guys, follow me," Kenji ordered and started to walk away.

Shimo, Daichi, Tai and I followed closely. After a few paces he turned to face us while walking backwards and said, "Whoa, hold up. Loosen up. You're supposed to be here to have fun, remember? Don't walk so...rigid. Chill."

We quickly did as ordered. Once Kenji was satisfied with our adjustment he turned back around and kept lecturing. "When you're on a mission you have to play the part. It doesn't matter if you're dressed as a maintenance man, window washer, waiter, or just being yourself in a crowd and trailing someone, you have to fall into the role set before you."

He continued to lead us out of the lower level where we initially entered and as I followed him I reflected on what Kenji had just said. He was right. Fall into the role. Play a part. And it occurred to me that maybe, someday, I would have to pretend to be someone that I wasn't just to get close to my target, lure him away, and carry out my orders.

Trickery.

It wasn't a very nice thing to have to do, but this was what we were being trained for. These were the lives we had chosen to lead.

We walked out into the busy plaza with its flashing lights, music thrumming, people bustling about shopping and children playing. Scents of chicken, beef, noodles, stir-fry, and just about any kind of seafood you could think of floated out into the plaza from the seven different restaurants laid out at the end. It made my stomach knot with instant hunger even though I had recently eaten. We crowded around Kenji as our group casually walked toward our goal. He paused at the skate park and pretended to enjoy watching the skateboarders do tricks off the ramps and rails. I watched him: his stance, his mannerism, how he carried himself. This was how we were expected to learn proper techniques - observing. Telling someone how to properly scan the area, or how to observe someone without making it look obvious honestly means nothing. But to *show* someone how to do it was the only way to make them fully understand. Visual training was always the best.

We spread out by the chain link fence that blocked off the skate park. Tai and Daichi were into the skaters. At least their parents let them have a board to skate from time to time. And I felt a little bitter towards Uncle for not allowing me to do the same. Shimo interacted with a guy close to our age and asked him to show us a few kick-flips while casually looking around.

"Duncan," he called to me as he balanced on the kid's board.

I walked over and pretended to be interested in what he was doing.

With his head down he mumbled, "There are two Shimoshuki scouts on the roof directly across from us." He then lost his balance and fell off the board.

I threw my head back and laughed, using the opportunity to look at the targets he indicated. Sure enough, two young men with the kanji symbol for strength, the Shimoshuki Clan symbol, were on the roof.

Kenji stepped over to us. "Nice call, Shimo," he said quietly. "Duncan, good scouting. You guys are using the area well." He walked over to Tai and Daichi then stopped short as something caught his attention.

Coming from the same direction of the parking garage was a small group of well-dressed men, sporting dark suits, sunglasses (at night?) and some wearing black driving gloves. In the midst of the pack, which consisted of several Shimoshuki, two dark-skinned Americans and a light-skinned man of unknown origin, was a blonde-haired man that appeared to be German. Short spiky blonde hair accented his pale, sharp features and though I couldn't get a good look, he seemed to be just a few inches taller than myself and very thin. The group strolled past us at a quick pace, ignoring looks and stares from the hordes of people enjoying the plaza, and continued on to The Jade Tree restaurant.

Kenji cast us a look, then turned and walked in the same direction. Our training instantly kicked in like it was second nature. Each of us instinctively knew what to do without being told. One by one we trailed behind, spanning our distance and doing our best to not look like we were together or following the group of men. Some of us paused at shop windows to look at electronics, some to glance at the latest Western fashion. Daichi walked with Kenji pretending to talk to someone on his cell phone. Things were going along great and it didn't seem like we were noticed at all.

Our target went inside the restaurant. We were to stay outside and observe the Shimoshuki scouts, watch what they were doing and make sure they didn't get aggressive. At least, that was the plan. Unfortunately plans had a way of being altered. This happened to be one of those times.

While stationed at the entrance of an alley that ran along the side of The Jade Tree I noticed movement in the shadows. A female figure clad all in black shifted from the building shadows, one after the other, and worked her way back to the end of the alley. Her long hair swished with her movements and from the faint lamplight I caught a glimpse of her face. Could it be? Jewel. My heart did flip-flops in my chest. If it was my sister, I wanted to talk to her; I missed her so much.

Instinctively I flattened my back against the wall and entered the dark, inching my way closer in pursuit of the mysterious female figure. Placing one foot across the other, and sinking into my knees, I made my way about half way down the alley. At first I lost sight of her until a trash can fell over and several cats ran past me in a panic. She then opened a door and ducked into the back entrance of the restaurant. I made for the door, but was stopped as three figures stepped out of the dark and into the dim moonlight blocking my path.

"Going somewhere?"

His voice told me he was as young as me, the height of their figures partially hidden in the dark revealed they were taller than me, one was thickly built, and the other two were thin. It wasn't until they stepped out into the light that I knew who they were – the three teens that attacked Hikaru and me several weeks ago.

"I don't think he's going anywhere. Are ya, freak?" The thick guy said in his deep voice, and just then something clicked in my brain. I knew him, and not from the initial attack, but more recently...

"Have any more secret late night outings?" I smirked, and then positioned my body, ready for a surprise attack.

"You know this guy?" Straggly Hair said unsnapping the thin black jacket he wore to reveal an arsenal of stars and kuni neatly tucked in pouches of the lining. He removed a few and positioned them in his hand.

"This is the one I told you about," Deep Voice said, nodding with his head towards me. "Don't let his elemental Earth energy latch onto your Air attacks. He all but drained my suto-mu." He scowled at me, obviously remembering our encounter in the woods a few nights ago.

"Ahhhh, the guy with special abilities, double swords, and apparently you have a friend that has special elemental powers too, don't ya?" Leader said, and suddenly flung a kuni my way.

The attack was flawless and quick, but with the slightest movement I evaded without adjusting my stance. I had to admit; I didn't even notice the knife as it had slid down his sleeve and rested in his hand. I had to be careful. They'd gotten a lot better since the last time we fought.

"By the way, we're looking for a friend of ours. A kunoichi. Name's Shi'tori. You know of her?" Straggly Hair said, while adjusting another kuni in his hand.

I kept a solemn expression; not letting on that the name struck a nerve. "What about the girl that just went inside?" I suggested.

"Oh, that's our secret weapon," Leader sneered.

"Doc said to take him alive," Deep Voice muttered to the others.

They eyed me up like I was a side of beef and grinned as if they had mischief and malice on their minds. Chills ran up my spine and I suddenly just wanted to get past them. What were they thinking?

Leader and Deep Voice suddenly engaged me, flinging stars at me while quickly approaching. Straggly Hair maneuvered his way behind me and pulled a kuni. I was surrounded in an instant. I dodged the stars without the use of a kuni; allowing them to whiz past using only subtle twists of my upper body. One nicked my cheek; another skimmed my hair removing a small strand. Other than that I was unscathed. I back kicked Straggly Hair in the gut, front snap kicked Leader in the chest and landed a back fist to Deep Voice's face. Gathering speed and calling on my Ki, I cleared the space between us by running along a small portion of the alley wall, jumped to the ground, made it to the back door of the restaurant and went inside.

The kitchen bustled with cooks shouting, pots and pans clanging and knives chopping. The aromas of many five-star dishes floated in the air as fine china clinked, while being passed from chef to chef. It was a small kitchen, but the hired help made do, skillfully sliding past each other. I needed to get past them and suddenly Kenji's words came to mind. Play the part, fit in. Blend. I moved forward into the crowd, twisted and turned as I grabbed an apron and put it on, donned a hat, and turned and dodged even more, instantly becoming an employee. I finally made it to the dining room entrance and grabbed a serving tray.

I entered the fancy dining room, placed a couple glasses of water on my tray and slowly made my way through the tables and chairs. I quickly located the Shimoshuki and their honored guest. Finding the mysterious woman that looked like Jewel was my next objective. If all went well I should be able to eavesdrop on the group's conversation, talk to my sister, get out the front entrance and join my team without being noticed. That was my plan at least, but as I said before, plans do have a way of getting altered.

Out of the many waitresses and waiters there was one that fit the description of the female shadow. She was clearing a table next to the Shimoshuki group. I worked my way over to her.

She kept her head turned away. I had a feeling she knew I was close by. Clanking and scuffling came from the kitchen. The three Shimoshuki teens emerged and the cooks were fussing at them. They scanned the dining area, but I turned away, hid my face and kept to my objective.

I inched my way closer, taking place mats from the empty table next to her and putting them on the cleared table where she was working. I was right up against her, completely invading her personal space.

"Ruby?" I whispered.

She didn't respond.

"Ruby is that you? Where have you been? I've missed you. Please come home soon."

She huffed and pushed past me, never letting me see her face. It was her, I was almost sure of it. Any one else would've looked at me and said they weren't Ruby. But what did Leader mean when he said she was their secret weapon? Was she here to protect the German guy? Were the rumors about my sister true? Had she connected with this foreigner and turned against her own people? My heart sank as I watched her gently push through the waitresses and enter the kitchen with a tub of dirty dishes.

My focus then centered on the Shimoshuki. Whatever the reason was for this foreigner's visit, it had something to do with the item the Chiao Village kept hidden and secret. He wanted it for his own personal gain – whatever the cost. The Shimoshuki were helping him for monetary rewards and the fact that they hated us and wanted to wipe us off the map.

Lately too many people had secrets, too many people were sneaking about, and I was coming to understand that it all filtered down to the Shimosuki and this foreigner. He had a connection to my sister, my family, and my people. *He* was the problem. And a sudden rage filled me as my gaze settled on him.

13
The Perfect Kill

"The whole idea is to not destroy them, but rather to scatter them," the foreigner said in a thick German accent, one that alluded he was high-classed. "Once they're out of the way we can simply walk in and take what we want."

"You mean, what *you* want," a dark-skinned American said, pointing an accusing finger at the German.

"Come now. The venture serves us all." The German was suave, smooth and very sure of himself.

I was only two steps away, setting the table directly across from them. Disguised as a waiter and standing so close, I felt sure I could slit his throat and vanish without a trace. With that thought in mind, I cautiously pulled a kuni from my jeans, palmed it and waited for the opportune moment.

"We've been listening to you go on and on about whatever it is in their village..." the other American snapped.

"And for what?" One of the Shimoshuki cut in. "You speak of capital gain, a new world order, blah, blah, blah. We don't even know what it is they have and neither do you! Well, *we* have an idea, but they've been entrusted with so many things from all over the world that we can't really be sure. And *you* don't know..."

"I have a pretty good idea, gentlemen. Now if you'll all please calm down I'll let you in on a bit of information," the German said.

Once the heated conversation subsided the German leaned back in his chair, taking on the poise of one completely in control. I moved around my table, taking in all that was said.

"What they have, gentlemen, is information." His eyes grew wide and his short spiky hair seemed to bristle with excitement; overall taking on the look of a mad man as he spoke. "Not just *any* information, but something that goes back to the ancients. I'm not sure what form it's in, but when I see it I'll know."

"How will we know it's the correct item when our men see it?" Another Shimoshuki said.

"Legend has it that what we seek is on parchment, in some form or another. It holds ancient Egyptian writing and hieroglyphics. You see, gentlemen, this item the Chiao hold actually is nothing more than a marker to an even greater power. But don't take it too lightly; the marker itself is a great power, as well." The German paused. All eyes were on him. They were captivated by his words, and his very presence commanded respect and order without any effort. I inched closer, now working on the table behind them. "Now I don't need to go into any further detail..."

"Oh, I think you do. Our price has just gone up," One of the Americans sneered, picking up a steak knife and leaning forward.

"Don't be too sure of yourself, my friend. I have only to give the signal and your whole family will be wiped out," the German said.

"You lie," he challenged.

"None of your people are even around to stop us," the other black American chimed in.

The German admired a ruby ring on his finger and rubbed a thumb over it. "A signal can come in various forms. And modern technology is such a wonderful commodity, don't you think?" He smiled viciously. The comment raised eyebrows around the table and the man with the steak knife released his hold and sat back.

I was now in a perfect position directly behind the German. I could easily reach around and slit his throat, or simply run my kuni right through the back of his head. I contemplated my next move. My orders were to stay outside and observe the Shimoshuki; not assassinate the target. But here I was lined up to do just that and I had to hesitate, an action that had caused me problems in the past. I didn't want to hesitate; I wanted to end this confrontation and all future problems brought on by this man, and I could do it – right now.

I took two steps closer; no one was paying attention to me. My gaze was fixed on my target as I continued to play the part of a causal waiter. The excitement of the kill raced in my heart, yet I was calm and in control of my actions on the outside. The kuni was poised; I lined up with the back of his head. If I struck now he would only pause in mid-sentence, the rest of his group would have no idea what happened, giving me time to move away and get out the front door without being noticed. Ever so slightly I drew back my arm, preparing to strike with the snake-like quickness I'd learned since I was a child. The opportunity was perfect...

More ruckus echoed from the kitchen, drawing my attention and forcing me to look up. The three Shimoshuki teens burst from the waitress station, ran through the dining room and out the front door. Kenji emerged from the kitchen and walked casually through the dining room, hands in his jeans pockets, while looking at me from the corner of his eye. His gaze settled on me.

I froze in mid-strike. Our eyes met. He gave me a hard stare, subtly shook his head, and then motioned for me to get outside.

The diners weren't looking at Kenji at all, they were still murmuring amongst themselves about the 'crazy boys that ran through the dining room.' It was a great cover and Kenji simply looked like someone who had finished eating and was leaving for the night, so no one even glanced his way. I had to do the same.

From where I stood I could see the hallway that led to the restrooms. I quietly backed away from the German and his group, slipped into the bathroom, removed my apron and hat and left. I paused at the front door for a final look back at the waitress station. Jewel wasn't there. If her presence was only to protect the German then why didn't she try to stop me from killing him? Perhaps she wanted me to kill him? Perhaps she simply left out the back door and didn't know what I was going to do? Perhaps, in some way, she was a prisoner, taking on a vow to him to protect those she loved? I shook the questions from my mind – they were too hurtful. Deep inside I knew she just couldn't be on the Shimoshuki's side. There had to be another reason.

I emerged into the chill early summer night air, spied Shimo not too far away and was suddenly grabbed by the back of my shirt. The force of the grip was fast and powerful and I knew right away it was Kenji.

He dragged me around the corner and into the alley then slammed my back against the building.

"What the hell were you doing?" he shouted, his nose only inches from mine.

"I could've done it; then all our problems would be over," I shouted back.

"You broke formation!"

"I saw my sister!"

"You what?" Kenji was suddenly dumbstruck.

"Jewel is here," I said in a quieter tone. "I saw her in the alley down there. When I went to talk to her she went in the kitchen door. Then those three jerks showed up. They threatened me. I got past them."

Kenji released his hold on me and stood quietly, waiting for me to finish. Everyone knew about Jewel and what she was being accused of. More than anything I wanted the allegations to be false.

"I just wanted to talk to her. That's all. I put on the apron and hat and went out on the floor. I tried to talk to her, but she hid her face and walked away, ignoring me. That's when I realized how close I was to that man. I could've finished him, Kenji."

"That's not your call, Duncan. Captain Yoshida has reason to believe that we still need *that man* alive a while longer," Kenji said, stabbing a finger in my chest.

"Why? He's causing the Shimoshuki to attack us more now than ever because of something we have, something no one will disclose to the rest of us. But I heard. That's right. I heard what they were saying and he disclosed some of what that special item was." I scowled and crossed my arms. "It would've been a good thing if I had killed him." I argued.

Kenji released a sigh of defeat and said in a quiet tone, "Yes, Duncan, it would be a good thing. But we can't act on our own because we feel our decision is a better one. We have to follow orders. You know the rules. You've never disobeyed an order before. Never." He paused, scowled then stepped closer to me. Lowering his voice he continued. "You're not to speak of the item we keep hidden and secret. Do you understand me? Not to your fellow Shinobi, Mayumi, your best friend, your reflection, no one. No exceptions. Got it?" His steely gaze bore into me – waiting for an answer.

Secrets. It was all part of being what we were – assassins – Shinobi – young modern-day warriors. The trust level had to be there. The will to keep information to yourself, control feelings about your actions and basically hold everything in. Yeah, I knew what he meant. This time, however, it was personal and I wasn't sure how to separate the two.

"Yes, sir," I finally muttered; not happy yet giving him the respect he deserved as our Team Leader.

Upon hearing my response his attitude softened. "Look, I know there's something eating at you about tonight. I think you need counsel over it," Kenji said, leading me out of the alley and signaling for the guys to regroup with us. "Duncan, you cannot let personal feelings interfere with your mission, no matter how subtle or easy a mission, no matter how difficult and involved a mission. We've all been trained for this. Suppress your feelings. Block them out and focus."

My throat was tight and my head was reeling over my sister's actions and how this German might be connected to her. I couldn't block it out. It hurt so much and I summed up that no amount of training could prepare me for something like this.

"Yeah, I know," was all I could choke out. He was right, and I knew it, but I didn't like it now that it touched my immediate family.

Just at that moment Kikaku and his team walked past us and headed toward the opposite end of the plaza. Makoto and his team were already at the far end, spread out and looking involved in a group of kids dancing to rap music. I watched Kikaku. Unfortunately during our entire mission he had been stationed elsewhere. It was a great opportunity for him to secretly meet with a Shimoshuki. And why not? It seemed everyone else was meeting with them, sneaking around, making deals and selling out our people. What the hell was going on? The fact that I couldn't figure it out burned a hole in my gut. The idea that the Shimoshuki had actually infested the minds of many of our young people was alarming. What were they doing? What were they planning?

The things the German said rang in my head and I tried to make sense of them, but it was too much at the moment. I would have to take Uncle's advice and meditate on it, just like he did when an answer to a situation eluded him. Meditation wasn't something I had much patience for, but this was something that would be worth it.

All of us eventually wound up blending with the dance group, mingling like we didn't know each other. Kenji stood next to Kikaku. Makoto joined them. I knew what they were doing and positioned myself far enough away, yet close enough to eavesdrop.

Hands in his pockets, head bobbing to the music and watching the kid's dance, Kenji quietly said, "Report."

"Nothing on my end," Makoto said, postured the same as Kenji. He always seemed to imitate him in a variety of ways.

"Where have you been?" Kenji asked Kikaku.

"With my team," Kikaku responded clenching his teeth.

"Twice you didn't respond when I called you on our microcomm."

"We observed Shimoshuki scouts on the streets. They didn't do anything suspicious," Kikaku said ignoring his statement. "They were packin' though. It seemed they were ready for some action."

"Well, we got intel," Kenji said, still keeping to the same quiet tone and not looking like he was talking to anyone in particular.

"Problems?" Makoto said.

"Just a slight, but no big deal. Duncan was actually the one that abstracted the information."

"Really? Has he told you yet?" Kikaku's voice wavered slightly, like he was nervous about something. I saw his eye twitch and he looked like he had to force a lump down with a hard swallow.

"Not yet," Kenji said. "But it's important information. I'll go with him to report to Captain Yoshida and Master Jun."

"We'll come, too," Kikaku volunteered.

"Not necessary..." Kenji's voice issued a warning.

"But won't hurt," Kikaku shot back with a mischievous grin.

There was tense silence between them, but I continued to stay close. That's when I saw Kikaku cast a glance at me from the corner of his eye, hold it, and a sly smile passed over his lips. He had plans for me and I was totally ready for the confrontation so I could beat his ass.

With slight signals only our team members knew, the Team Leaders ordered us to fall back and return to our transports. All of us did just that, and as we left we noticed that the German and his Shimoshuki group had left The Jade Tree and were walking down the row of shops several feet in front of us. Unfortunately, we had to act like we didn't see them.

Suddenly, an alarm went off inside my head and a shiver ran up my spine, the kind that instinctively told me I was being watched. I looked up, directing my gaze to the rooftops. There, perched on the edge just above the German, was a kunoichi, dressed in tight-fitting black with a katana strapped to her back. Her long dark hair stirred slightly in the breeze. It *was* Jewel. Our eyes locked. She inclined her head slightly then moved away. My eyes didn't leave her as she ran along the rooftops, leaping over breaks, light as a feather, swift as air, keeping up with the entourage and just slightly ahead of them. She flipped off a building, glided down the awning of a local coffee shop, gently landed on the ground by the parking garage and disappeared into the shadows, just as the Shimoshuki entered to collect their vehicles.

Our brief moment of contact lingered in my mind all the way back to Master Jun's Night Ops training area. We met with them in the large indoor training building stocked like a dojo and gym, but with ladders, levels and ropes hanging from the rafters. Only a small portion was Master Jun's office. Master Jun, Captain Yoshida and my uncle, as well as several men from the Black Dragon Squad greeted us. They were ready for my report. All eyes were on me, especially Kikaku. I was nervous. What was I going to say? Should I tell them everything? To spill information about my sister would condemn her. If it was found out that I withheld information I could be punished and considered a conspirator, as well. I couldn't lie. Of course, for a ninja there was no such thing as an actual lie, it was all about how you arranged your words.

I stood at attention before the group of three. The others stood back from me.

"Now, then, Duncan, why don't you begin by telling us why you broke formation without telling your Team Leader!" Captain Yoshida snapped.

Kenji was standing away from me; hands clasped behind his back, and cringed when the captain raised his voice. Apparently he knew what I was up against.

"I was stationed at the opening of an alley, sir." Not a lie. "I noticed movement in the alley." A slight exaggeration.

"And?" Captain Yoshida sounded impatient.

"At first I wasn't sure what it was." I skirted around the answer.

"Duncan, you don't have to be nervous. All members must report their actions and what was seen and heard when returning from a mission. This is only basic procedures," Master Jun gently assured me. "Now, continue."

"It was a kunoichi..." I choked out.

"Chasing women?" Master Jun raised an eyebrow and cast an amused glance at Uncle.

"No, sir. It was my sister."

All joking aside. Mumbled conversation hummed among those standing around.

"Are you sure?" Master Jun's voice was a little tense.

"Pretty positive." I tried not to sound too positive.

"Hmmm, I see." Captain Yoshida grunted and turned to Uncle. "Ruby had been under your care since Kato and Anju were murdered, Tou-Pang."

"She's a grown woman, Captain. She must be responsible for her own actions," Uncle said stiffly, not meeting the captain's hard stare.

Captain Yoshida simply grunted. I started to wonder what was actually going on between those two. They had respect for each other and it seemed like they had been friends at one time, but something about my sister and me put them at odds. I knew that my past violent actions had the captain ready to carry out a threat against me, but what was the real deal with Ruby? She didn't kill the German and she didn't try to stop me from killing him. That had to count for something. After a brief silence and shuffling of papers Master Jun motioned for me to continue.

"I entered the alley with the intent to talk to her. I was intercepted by three teen Shimoshuki – the same three that attacked Hikaru and me several weeks ago."

The three men cast glances at each other, but I continued anyway.

"I eluded their attacks, got past them and went into the restaurant only because I wanted to speak to my sister." Not a lie. "Once inside I disguised myself as a waiter, walked out on the floor and approached her."

"Did she speak?" Uncle questioned, looking hopeful.

"No, sir." I said flatly, still feeling the hurt from her rejection. "She didn't acknowledge me and walked away. That's when I realized how close I was to the German and the Shimoshuki. So, I hung around and eavesdropped on their conversation."

"Very good, Duncan," Master Jun praised, and then nodded for me to continue.

"The German was talking. He said he only wanted to scatter us, not really destroy us. That way they could just walk into our village and take the item he wanted so badly."

"What item is this?" Master Jun said.

"I don't really know." A lie. I glanced at Kenji. He raised an eyebrow at me. "The German said it was a marker for an even greater power. Even he didn't know exactly what it looked like, but he had some sort of an idea."

Partial lie. I didn't want to say that it was in parchment form. I was sure Captain Yoshida knew what the item was, and it was clear to me that Uncle knew, but what about everyone else standing around and listening in, especially Kikaku, who watched me like a hawk?

"And it seemed this German had control over the Shimoshuki and Americans."

"How so?" Uncle said.

"One of the men picked up a steak knife and threatened their guest. The German said all he had to do was give a signal and that man's entire family would be wiped out," I said, which was totally the truth. "The man believed him and backed down."

Uncle, Master Jun and Captain Yoshida exchanged troubled looks.

"That's all for now, Duncan. You may go," Captain Yoshida ordered.

Kenji came up to me and nodded for me to follow him. I did

just that. As I passed Kikaku, he caught me by the upper arm, squeezed and pulled me close.

"You're a problem," he growled low in my ear so no one else would hear.

"Get your hands off me, jerk," I growled back.

"We'll just have to take care of your attitude," he threatened.

"Try it," I challenged.

"Hey! Break it up," Kenji said trying to come between us, but Kikaku wouldn't have it.

A kuni came out of nowhere, an overhead strike with the blade aimed for my face. Instinctively I blocked with a kuni of my own. The sharp, metal blades clashed with a metallic ring and held firm as the room fell silent. We held our positions, internally struggling against each other's will and externally with our might. Our eyes locked, his grip on my arm tightened and strangely enough Kikaku started to smile.

The timely appearance of Captain Yoshida and two Black Dragons stopped Kikaku. However, he didn't seem all that bothered by their presence as he backed off and pocketed his kuni. Instead, he physically challenged them without uttering a word; puffing out his chest and tightening his arm muscles. The Dragons moved on him, closing in on either side. Kikaku released his hold on me at that point and Captain Yoshida pushed between us, chest to chest with Kikaku - though he was much shorter - and grunted loudly, with nostrils flaring, eyes wide and face red with anger. It was practically an order without the use of words. He was angry as hell.

Kikaku backed away, turned and brushed past the Dragons, shrugging off their attempt to take hold of his arms. He then flashed stepped out into the night. The Dragons turned to pursue, but the captain put out his arm and halted their attempt.

"Let him go," Captain Yoshida said. "He will be dealt with."

14
Power of the Elementals

The next few days were uneventful. Early weapons training became more and more difficult and challenging. We expanded on working with more than one weapon, losing our weapons in mid-fight and having to use whatever was at our disposal, as well as fighting a multitude of opponents blindfolded. And every day Master Katsumi reminded me that we would start special night training just as soon as he could get his schedule rearranged. I was beginning to wonder if we would ever get started.

Hikaru continued to drag through each day looking bleary-eyed, like he had used up every ounce of Ki left in his body. I hung out with him as much as possible until he started to come up with lame excuses for why we couldn't do things together after dinner. It was becoming more difficult to communicate with him and it seemed he just didn't have much to say anymore. I watched Hikaru slip away from me and I couldn't even figure out why, but I knew it had something to do with his late night excursions.

My mind drifted back to the night I followed a shadow into the forest, far from our village, and witnessed what I thought was

Hikaru fighting what turned out to be an American ninja. Had it really been him? Did I interrupt training instead of a real fight? And why was he taking special and secret training with someone outside our village?

It was common knowledge to anyone in The Field that the Chiao Village trained the best assassins and spy-warriors in the world. So, why would an outsider train him? As it was, I broke up the battle, executed my new move on the smaller ninja and then he got away. I never did find out if it was really Hikaru. The only proof I had was that the next day Hikaru complained his back hurt. My attack had that effect on people, but it wasn't enough to go on. I wanted to follow him again, but each night afterwards Uncle had kept a close watch on me. It was frustrating, and during the days that followed I had to act like I had nothing better to do than hang out at the house until Uncle backed off.

The other opposition was Kikaku. More than once he'd let me know how much he hated me and wanted Mayumi for himself. Now, after our last incident at the debriefing from the recent Night Ops mission it's become apparent he's made me his target. Kikaku was a problem. I could see it. Why couldn't Kenji and Makoto? After our training mission I had felt Kenji and Makoto were coming around and starting to respect me, possibly treating me more like an equal. They definitely showed me a grown-up and professional side that I'd never seen before. Hopefully that attitude would continue. I just couldn't understand why they insisted on hanging out with Kikaku. Maybe it was because the three of them were pre-Black Dragons and would be entering The Trials together?

Either way, things were pretty messed up. I sat quietly on the front porch trying my best to meditate over it, but answers eluded me. I had to be patient and think things through; at least, that's what Uncle always said. If I rushed to an answer I could embarrass myself by making false accusations. The whole thing was very frustrating, but still I tried. I squirmed and fidgeted in place, trying to get more comfortable, then took a deep breath, released it slowly and tried again.

Then there was this whole thing about several teens running around late at night. Hikaru and Kikaku were part of that issue, as well. How many were actually running around at night no one knew, not even Morgan. Although Morgan had great insight as to what was going on, more than I did, and always seemed to show up and give me information just when I needed it. How he knew when to do that I still couldn't figure out. I guess it would be best to just not worry about it. It was quite clear Morgan was on my side, which was way cool. The thought comforted me and I took another deep breath, feeling my lungs fill, and then released the air slowly.

That's when my mind cleared slightly and a comment Morgan made to me only days ago resurfaced. He mentioned that the Shimoshuki were teaching their teens how to tap into their animal style of fighting, which made them crave to use it even more; this caused them to become very aggressive. Perhaps using this technique was releasing endorphins, or an addictive chemical in the brain, causing them to react differently than we did? We hadn't learned our animal fighting style just yet, but it was coming soon. I felt this was a subject I needed to talk to Uncle about.

The other thing Morgan said that intrigued me was the part about a legendary assassin named Master Tsubasa from the Tesenga Clan that was long gone. I couldn't figure out why he would inform me of this, but Morgan didn't tell me anything unless it was important. So, maybe I needed to know that the Shimoshuki had gotten in touch with this man for whatever reason? Maybe, in some way, it involved me? Maybe it was because I'd had entirely too many run-ins with those three Shimoshuki teens in such a short period of time?

That brought up another question. What did the Big Guy mean when he said, 'Doc said for us to take him alive'? The thought of what he meant immediately sent shivers up my spine, just like it did the night of our encounter. Once again, those guys seemed to have made me their target.

"Duncan?" The voice was soft, a subtle intention, but I brushed it away; I didn't want to leave my inner shadow world.

I was so deep into my thoughts I felt like I was no longer breathing, yet sitting on a pillow of air in a gray realm. I liked this. Alone with my thoughts. Meditation wasn't so bad after all.

"Duncan?" The voice was louder and a bit more annoying this time. Several pokes in the shoulder pulled me back to the present. "Helllooo."

I opened my eyes to find Shinji stooped down and staring me in the face.

"Dude! S'bout time. I've been trying to get your attention for a good five minutes," he said, flipping his bo staff around his hands like it was a twig.

"Aw, geez! I almost forgot," I said, wiping a hand over my face. I stood and stretched.

"How long were you under this time?" Shinji said. Ever since he assisted me in the forest fighting the big Shimoshuki teen he and I had been in closer contact with each other and he knew my daily routine. Meditating every day to reach a level of control was important, so he could teach me a new technique - and he was slowly taking Hikaru's place at my side.

"I think an hour," I speculated, "but let's get going. Oh, hold up a minute." I stuck my head in the door and shouted, "Uncle, I'm going to go train with Shinji now. Okay?" He muttered acknowledgement and gave me a gentle threat not to be late for dinner.

With Shinji at my side, we ran through the woods and entered the clearing that I had considered my secret special spot. Of course it wasn't so secret anymore; Mayumi knew about it and so did a few other boys that came here to work out alone. I was relieved to see that no one had already claimed the clearing once we got there.

"Okay, how are we gonna do this?" I stood across from Shinji and drew my swords.

"You want to learn how to channel your Ki into your swords without getting angry, right?" he said.

"Yeah."

"And I see you've really been working on your meditation, which should help."

"How did you learn?" I wanted him to get to the point.

"Well it didn't have anything to do with getting totally pissed and flipping out, if that's what you mean," Shinji laughed and held his bo staff center and at arms length. "And I can't tell you who taught me, either. So, don't ask."

"I figured as much," I thought back to the possibility of Hikaru getting special training with an American ninja, someone outside our village. In a way I felt left out and a bit envious, but soon I would be getting special training from Master Katsumi - whenever he could find the time to begin. In the mean time I had Shinji and this was our special secret training for the moment.

"Okay, first let me explain. As you know our Ki is our energy. We have specific energy points throughout our body, and you know as well as I do that all we have to do is touch a point on our opponent and we screw up their energy flow."

"Right. It can totally throw them off balance and you gain the advantage in the fight," I finished.

"Exactly." Shinji repositioned his bo staff at center and in front of his chest. "These energy points can also extend to our weapon. Master Katsumi harps on our weapons being an extension of ourselves and that we can use our ninpo to channel our Ki through our punches or kicks to promote some pretty astonishing results."

"Yeah, like my first day in weapons class when I blew apart the dummy with a simple kick." I

couldn't help a smirk.

"Oh, yeah, I heard about that," he laughed a goofy sort of laugh. "That was awesome." After a few giggles and snorts he then cleared his throat and got serious again. "Anyway, let's do this." He slowly blew out a breath, ran the fingers of his left hand down the left side of the bo staff and immediately an orange glow, like soft flames, ignited all around the tip. He twirled the staff, and then slapped the flaming end down hard on the ground. A burst of energy shot forward and blew past me, leaving a thin burned trail in its wake.

I looked at my blades and said, "Okay, so how did you do that?"

"All I did was tap into my Ki. I used ninpo to focus it out past my hand and into the bo staff. It's a type of ninja magic we all possess. You did the same thing the other night, but you were in your, well, your Power Form I guess we could call it. You need to do this without being under that type of influence. If you can achieve this, then you may be able to suppress your other side and have more control over your anger."

"Makes sense." I felt a bit hopeful. "So, why is your energy orange?"

"The Ki that I'm using is actually my elemental energy, which is Earth. When I first saw it I wondered why it wasn't green, like the Earth, but that's not how it works. If you look closely..." he raised his staff tip so I could look at the glowing energy radiating from the end. "This isn't actually fire, its power. See? It looks like a pack of dogs running, doesn't it?"

I squinted at the strange figures moving throughout the glow. "What is it, actually?"

"Wolves. That's my inner animal, my animal fighting style. That's why I call my attack Wolf's Bane." His face was alight with pride. "Each one is different and each person has a slightly different color for their animal Ki, or elemental energy. Now, seeing you wig out the other night, I've figured that your animal fighting style is the dragon, your elemental energy is fire."

"Wow, that night I decided to call my attack Dragon Claw," I added.

"Exactly. See how it all fits? When you call on the energy it all comes together in a matter of seconds. Your Ki taps into your elemental energy, which, in turn, is used to tap into your animal fighting style, then, as you use your ninpo it assists in projecting your elemental energy into your weapon and beyond," Shinji said, taking a breath. "Everyone training as a Shinobi eventually learns this, but I'll teach you now because I think it'll help you."

Good ole Shinji. He had such a big heart. I was amazed at how advanced he was and still not doing anything with it, well, other than teaching me.

"Where'd my blue flame color come from?" I said, referring to my energy glow. "Shouldn't it be red?"

"I dunno. That's just the way you are," he shrugged. "Come on. Let's get to work or you'll be late for dinner."

I rolled my eyes, but couldn't help a small grin.

"Now, it doesn't take raw force to do this. Just nudge your focus to tap into your inner animal. You'll find it hidden just below the sternum yet close to your heart. Then adjust the flow of

Ki to your fingertips and down the blade." He demonstrated with the bo staff and I saw a flicker of orange along its length "Now you try, but maybe you should start with only one sword."

I returned one sword to the holder on my back and took on a fighting stance.

"Don't be so rigid. Relax a little." Shinji tapped my leg with the bo staff and I felt a little of the heat. "Even in a fight you don't have to be so tense."

"You sound like Master Katsumi." I relaxed my stance and held my sword with the right hand, the left lightly touching the base of the blade, and breathed. I found my inner animal right where Shinji said it would be. It was a swirling mass of energy, pulsing with life, churning, pulling apart and reforming. I took hold of it, directed it, and then found my Ki, seated in the center – and a warm presence -

I've been waiting...

I ignored the voice. I didn't want Shinji to know about it. Instead I called on my Ki, mixed it with my inner animal, and allowed the warmth of my energy to flow through my body, down my arms and into my fingertips. That's when the voice became louder and more persistent.

Let me out...

I felt the energy stop as it extended just beyond my fingertips and touched the blade, as if it were blocked. I pushed a little more.

Let me live...

"Come on, Duncan, you can do it. You're right there. Take it from your fingertips and up the blade. Here, let me try something. You just need a little encouragement," Shinji said and leveled his bo staff at me.

Kill everything!

I suddenly felt sick to my stomach and bowed my head to my

blade, trying to force the Ki to flow down the blade like I did several nights ago. Maybe the Ki blockage was making me sick? Hearing the voice wasn't helping. Shinji was ready to spar and help me attune to this new ability and I couldn't even finish up.

Shinji tapped my blade with his staff. "Come on. Fight me," he said playfully.

"Damn it!" I spat. My head swam, I wanted to retch and couldn't; the voice chanted nonsense in my ears and I couldn't control my Ki. For the first time ever I couldn't make it go where I wanted it. I never had this problem before. Why?

Don't you know?

"Hey buddy, you okay?' Shinji tried to lift up my chin to look at my face.

A surge of power took over me like a tremendous shiver and advanced throughout my body. My head came up, my eyes snapped open and Shinji was now my enemy.

Death. Death to all so new life may take hold, I thought, but it wasn't my thought.

"Duncan? Dude, your eyes - they're black again." He took a few steps back. Fear radiated off of him and I absorbed the smell through my skin and a devilish smile rose to my lips. "Why are you smiling at me like that? You hardly ever smile. Duncan? You hear me?"

My blade ignited in a burst of soft blue flame, not just the tip, but the entire blade. I squared off. My sights set on the target before me.

Shinji ignited the other end of his bo staff and expanded the energy field down most of the ends. His stance told me he was ready to face death.

15
Chains of Fate

We circled each other slowly, trying to decide who should attack first. I wanted to spill his blood, see his death and the thought of it made my inner soul ache to bring it into being, but still I paused and waited. He hesitated and said something that I couldn't understand, yet could only piece together a few discernable words. It all resonated like foreign echoes in my head. My consciousness lifted out of the black void and into the gray.

What is happening to me? I was confused as to what my body was doing.

Again I entered the black void just as quickly as the gray and focused on my target. The taste of his fear excited me; it pulsed under my skin. Frustration. Still I waited.

"Duncan, you're not yourself right now." Shinji stayed low, staff ready. "It's me. Shinji. Remember? I don't want to hurt you." He twirled his staff, the energy on the tips hummed in the air.

The human talked. It was annoying, like the buzzing of flies. I moved my blade over my left shoulder, swished it carelessly out in front of me and cast out a rope of energy. He dodged it. Several more quick ropes. He rolled away from those. He must die.

I entered the gray void again and heard Shinji reasoning with me. *I have to stop!* The black void pulled me down once again and just before I went under Shinji's voice rang in my ears.

"Duncan, try to remember who I am," Shinji panted and struggled to his feet. "I know you're in there. Come on. You gonna let that thing have control over you?"

I drew back my arm to cast the Dragon Claw. Power surged up my arm; the blue flame grew and fingered out into the air, taking on a life of its own.

Yes....

Just one swift motion and he would fall. The gray void surfaced. Suddenly, my head hurt, an inexorable throbbing pulsed behind my eyes and I paused. The pain almost brought me to my knees, but then the gray void bled into light. Shinji came into focus. What was I doing?

Do it....

Wait! No. What was going on?

Don't defy me...

I closed my eyes, squinted tightly and moaned. "Shinji." I put my hand to my head and reeled but didn't lose balance. "Shinji. I can't do this."

"It's okay, Duncan." He still kept his distance from me.

You are my vessel...

"Duncan, remember your meditation. Use it quickly."

Without hesitation I obeyed. I plopped on the ground; breathed, relaxed and suppressed the voice yet held tight to my Ki, not letting it slip away. Somehow it linked to the voice inside me.

No!..Noooo!...

I couldn't take that voice anymore, but I didn't want to tell Shinji about it. I had to push it away, hide it in a dark place inside me. *Breathe. Breathe. Calm, reach for the calm.*

After several moments I finally opened my eyes.

"Duncan? That you again?"

"Yeah, it's me." I focused on his face, my head cleared and I felt fully in control. "Hey, I still have my elemental energy on my blade." I cast a quick look at my sword showed it to him.

"You sure you're okay?" Shinji took several steps closer, yet wavered.

"I'm sorry, Shinji. I didn't hurt you, did I?"

"What happened?"

"I sort of lost myself, I guess. The anger inside of me it, well, it sort of took over. It was so easy and quick this time. I didn't know who you were. I only knew that I wanted to destroy all life," I shook my head.

"Why would you want to do that?"

"So new life would take its place."

"That's a whole lot of trouble to go through just to start all over," he said.

"I guess so. Don't worry about it. It was just one of many crazy thoughts rolling around in my head at the time. I think I dug too deep to get to my inner animal and Ki. Normally the Ki is always right there on the surface, but I wanted to do the technique correctly and I guess I over did it."

"You think you woke up that inner demon thing?" Shinji asked.

"Something like that." I stood away from him and stared at my sword, the gentle blue flames danced lightly along the edge of the blade, swirling and writhing like a coiled dragon with its many scales glimmering in the light. What was happening to me?

Shinji gave a little laugh and said, "Look at it this way. At least you found out what not to do. Better to find out now instead of finding out in front of everyone you train with."

I looked at Shinji and my expression softened. It was clear to my heart that he was a Shinobi I could trust with my life and all my secrets.

"Thanks, Shinji," I walked over to him and placed my hand on his shoulder. We stood silent for a moment. "You think we could work out for a while before I have to go home? I'll have to hold back though and not over do it."

"Yeah, sure, let's get busy."

For the next hour Shinji trained me to strike and block with my elemental energy while using my dragon fighting style. Using all of my acrobatics I learned how to throw a rope of energy while doing a flip, back roll and even catapulting off trees while running. It became so easy to execute and I didn't hear the voice in my head, nor did I feel its presence any more that day. We walked back to my house afterwards to find Uncle sitting on the porch waiting for us.

"I'm not late, Uncle, I'm right on time," I said in my own defense, just in case he was going to punish me. I couldn't take any more of Uncle's punishments.

"I'm just taking in the wonderful evening," he said, slyly.

Shinji picked up on the underlying meaning in his tone and said, "See ya, Duncan."

"Thanks for the workout."

We tapped fists, he left and I then turned my attention to Uncle.

"All right you sly old fox, what do you want now?" I raised an eyebrow, clearly suspicious as I sat in the chair next to Uncle.

"You know, we never had a thorough talk after you came back from your first active Night Ops Training." He leaned forward, fist on his thigh, eyes bright with mischief and dropped his voice. "I know you overheard things from the meeting. I also know you weren't telling all of the details during your debriefing. You said Jewel was there and you had dealings with her. Now, tell me what you found out."

I leaned back in my chair, crossed my arms across my chest and stretched out my long legs. Now, here was an interesting situation. Uncle wants me to tell him everything I know about that meeting, yet he refuses to tell me what it is the Chiao Clan kept secret and hidden that the Shimoshuki are willing to kill for. I pondered over this dilemma for a few seconds before responding and a slight smile actually touched the corner of my mouth.

"How about an exchange of information?" I finally said feeling empowered.

"Don't try to be slick, young man," Uncle said sternly.

"I just think it's fair..."

"Duncan, don't..." He rapped his knuckles on the table in protest, but I took it as frustration.

"Okay, okay." I paused and let out a deep breath, biding for time. "Well, you know, I really didn't hear all that much."

He sucked in a deep breath through his nose and narrowed his eyes at me. Normally this look would make me cringe, but not this time. I had a golden opportunity and I was not going to let him intimidate me into spilling my guts. I stood my ground. Several seconds went by as we held each other's gaze, silently challenging and not giving an inch.

Finally his face took on a relaxed expression. As he sat back in his chair he said, "Very well, let's do it your way."

My stomach did flip-flops with excitement. I won! Yes! Wait a minute - this could be a trap. Now his crafty ninja mind was working over time and he was most likely setting me up. I had to be careful, or I would tell him everything and he would reveal nothing. I took the plunge and applied negotiation tactics on him.

"Hmmm, well, okay, I'll ask a question, and then you ask a question. How about that?" I suggested.

"Very well."

"What is it we keep hidden and secret?" I said in a very determined fashion.

"Well, *we* don't disclose our secret entrances of this house,"

Uncle said, smiling with satisfaction.

"What? No! Not we as in you and I. I mean we as in the Chiao."

"You did not specify. My turn."

"What! Hey, that's not fair!"

"It's perfectly fair. You asked a question and I answered it. Now my turn."

He got me. I blew it. Damn!

"What did Jewel say to you?"

I pursed my lips, grumbling inside at how he quickly manipulated the situation back in his favor. "She didn't say anything." Uncle looked at me questioningly. "Serious. She ignored me even though I was right up in her face. When I called her by her name she didn't even look at me. She just walked away." I leaned forward in my chair and said, "Where does the Chiao keep the item that is secret?"

"Why do you want to know?"

I frowned. "You can't answer a question with a question."

"That wasn't part of our agreement."

Crap! He did it again.

I sighed and reluctantly said, "Because it's at risk of being found and stolen – for that German."

"Hmmm, this is a grave matter," Uncle stood and walked inside.

"Hey, you didn't answer my question!" I got up and trailed after him.

He quickly went to work in the kitchen, getting out plates and filling them with rice, vegetables and pork.

"Uncle, you need to answer my question," I persisted.

He abruptly turned and shoved a plate of food at me. "It's in the third building to the right."

"What's that supposed to mean?"

"One question at a time," Uncle took his plate and sat at the table. "My turn." I sat across from him and waited as he finished chewing. "Kenji told me in confidence that while you were spying on the German and his guests you were about to run him through."

"That's not a question. That's a statement."

"Oh, I know. What I want to know is where Jewel was while this was happening?"

"She wasn't around."

"At all?"

"Nope. At first I thought she was there to protect him, but she wasn't around when I was ready to kill him. Then, when we were leaving, she was up on the rooftops keeping an eye on him from a distance, pacing herself with the group as they went to their cars. It looked like a protective position, but then again, maybe it wasn't." I paused and cocked my head to the side. "Why?"

He didn't answer right away. With elbows on the table, something he normally didn't do, he sighed and rubbed his hands together. "I've been trying to figure out what Jewel is up to. It seems she's on her own personal mission; however, dark happenings are revolving around her involvement with this man."

"Uncle, I know he's linked to our family in some way. You need to tell me why. Ruby keeps hanging around him for whatever reason. He's responsible for the Shimoshuki attacking us now more than ever. Whatever we have, he wants so he can find another item of even greater power. For some reason he feels it will help him achieve his goal, which from what I've pieced together, may result in world domination. More than anything, I want to know if he has anything to do with my parent's deaths."

"You need to stay away from this man. I can't lose you like I've lost your sister..."

"You haven't lost her..."

Uncle threw up his hands. "We don't know whose side she's truly on!"

Our little game had suddenly turned very serious. Silence fell between us and I stared at him, too dumbstruck for words.

"What are you saying?" I couldn't believe what he was insinuating.

"There is talk that she's turned against us. That she can't be trusted..."

"I don't believe that..."

"Neither do I. But as Shinobi we must keep ourselves open to all possibilities, especially when it hits so close to home."

Kenji's words came to mind and a sick feeling churned in my stomach as I realized how right he was. When you're involved in a mission it's hard to keep emotions separate from what needs to be done, when it comes to people close to you. When it came right down to it, would I be able to arrest my own sister? Would I be able to kill her if given the task? My head drooped and my shoulders sagged at the thought.

"Duncan," Uncle's words came gently from across the table, our food now forgotten and cold. "I know this is difficult for you. She helped me raise you since you were a baby. You've always been close to her."

"Then she started to go away. Met that man. Started staying away longer and longer each time until she just didn't come back at all," I mumbled more to the table than to him.

"I know deep in your heart you blame her for the way you are; that maybe if she'd been here the whole time you wouldn't have an anger problem. It's not her fault," he said.

"I don't blame her anymore, Uncle. I know it's not her fault. But it is her fault for not being around for special days in my life." Hurt and misery leaked from my voice as I lifted my head to look at him. His eyes softened and I stood. "Dinner was wonderful, but I'm not very hungry right now. I'm going to go see Mayumi before it gets too dark. I'll be back soon."

He didn't protest as I slipped on my tabi boots and headed out the door.

16

Silent Edge

Twilight filtered through the sky and settled over the village as I walked to Mayumi's house. With summer approaching the days were getting longer and warmer, but the evenings were still cool. It was perfect to sit outside with my special girl and talk about her day, especially since I hadn't been able to talk to her for the past few days. We had some catching up to do and I was looking forward to it, anything to take my mind off the present situation.

I wound my way through backyards and around homes, by-passed side streets and skirted around a portion of Main Street that took me past the Flaming Dragon Pub. On nights like this the front door was propped open and I cast a glance inside as I continued on my way. Many of the older men from our village were there, drinking, laughing and talking so loudly all of Japan could hear them. I saw a few Black Dragons sitting quietly inside having a beer, as well as Master Katsumi and Akira's father sitting alone and in deep conversation. Both had serious looks on their faces, as if they were discussing a grave matter, and I noticed that Akira's father had a black eye and bloody lip. I raised an eyebrow at how unusual that was, especially since he was a highly trained ex-police officer. But I shook off the question and moved on to Mayumi's.

A little further down the street was an alley that I used as a short cut to her house. Narrow like a tunnel and surrounded by buildings, the alley was quiet with no one around. Just as I turned to cut through a figure emerged from around the corner at the far end. It was Kikaku. I froze in my tracks.

He casually leaned against the building and smiled mockingly at me, while pulling on a pair of thin black gloves. The action was a silent threat. "You and I have some unfinished business."

"I've got nothing to say to you." Every muscle in my body tightened instantly.

Kikaku slowly approached me yet kept a measure of distance between us. "You've gotten entirely too nosy lately. Are you trying to play Black Dragon?" He pulled out a kuni and flipped it around his fingers, looking at it thoughtfully as if he were testing the metal, *flip, flip, flip, stop, flip, flip, flip, twirl.* He skillfully rested the handle in his gloved hand after twirling it around one finger.

"Can't handle the pressure?" I didn't move from my position and waited for him to come to me.

"You know," he struggled with his sentence as if trying to find the right words, "I find it difficult to have someone looming over me."

"Tell that to someone who cares."

"I'm not going to warn you again – mind your own business!"

"What exactly do you have to hide?" I pressed the matter, hoping to get him to let slip some useful information. But Kikaku was a pre-Black Dragon; he wasn't going to be so careless.

"There's nothing..."

"Liar!"

With the help of his flash step, Kikaku was on me in a second. I anticipated the attack and sidestepped, grabbed him by the back of his shirt, took hold of his neck, then forced his upper body to bend forward and, at the same time, drove my knee into his gut. He choked out a painful cry, but recovered quickly. He brought the kuni up to run me through. I blocked, executed a palm strike to his chin so hard I heard his neck crack, and then landed a rapid succession of punches to his mid-section. Without pause, I hit him with a front snap kick so hard his back slammed into the building nearby forcing some of the wood to splinter, while leaving a slight imprint of his outline.

I jumped back into a fighting stance and waited to see what he'd do next.

"Back off, Kikaku," I warned. I felt like I'd made my point.

Holding his position against the building, Kikaku laughed. It started off as a soft chuckle then quickly built into a loud maniacal cackle.

"Or what?" he said. "You have no idea who you're dealing with, or what I can do to you."

He thrust forward his hand as if to grab me, though he was several feet away. With his hand still extended Kikaku slowly curled his fingers inward like he was grasping an invisible something in the air. There was nothing there, but the air started to feel heavy around me, suffocating, and in the midst of the sun still going down, the shadows thrown off by the surrounding buildings seemed to close in on me. My chest felt tight; it was becoming harder to breathe and though I backed away, the feeling wouldn't.

Though I didn't have the breath to answer, a voice from behind me rang out. "No, but I do!" And a streak of white energy shot past and deflected Kikaku's hand.

It was Akira, standing tall and proud with his kama ready. White energy gently swirled around the tips of his weapons.

Kikaku yelped and cradled his hand. "You again," he sneered and thrust out his other hand toward Akira, who stung that one with a white streak of energy, as well.

With Kikaku distracted the heavy feeling shrouding me suddenly lifted, but I felt a bit nauseous and dizzy and swiped at the sweat dripping down my face. I bent forward, rested my hands on my knees and panted for air while Akira dealt with him.

"Using the Dark Arts is not acceptable, Kikaku," Akira warned. "Captain Yoshida will be very interested to know how skilled you are. Where did you learn it? How much do you know?"

Still favoring his hand, Kikaku shifted his eyes from side to side, as if looking for an escape, then took a step back. The three of us were in a narrow alley, caught between buildings with one way in and one way out, unless you counted going straight up. Where Kikaku thought he was going to run was an interesting question. To me it appeared Akira had the upper hand. With kama poised to deflect another attack, Akira approached him with long, determined strides. Kikaku backed into the shadow of a building and seemingly disappeared. It wasn't a difficult trick; it was taught to us at an early age, but the way Kikaku did it looked unnatural and creepy. In the blink of an eye he was gone.

Akira rushed into the shadow; most likely hoping Kikaku was still there and only cleverly concealed. He wasn't. Annoyed, Akira kicked at the ground. He then approached me and slapped me on the back. The force made me stagger a bit.

"You all right?" He actually looked concerned. Maybe our little excursion to the old mill was a good thing after all.

"Yeah. Thanks," I said, and flashed him a grateful look. "What in the world was he doing to me?"

"Not sure, but it was the Dark Arts. I found out he knew how to execute that particular technique just last week when I caught him meeting with a stranger in the garage. He tried to do the same thing to me, but as soon as I staggered out into the sunlight the feeling went away. He and the guy he met with ran off before I could kick his ass." Akira paused and motioned for me to walk with him. I didn't protest; we were heading in the direction of Mayumi's house. "After talking to my aunts and uncles I found out what it was he did to me."

"But exactly what kind of Dark Technique?" I said, "We're not taught that kind of thing. It's unethical, though others think it's fair to use in battle." I thought back to Shi'tori and how she tried to convince Mayumi there was nothing wrong with the Dark Ninja Arts.

"There's been a lot of debate over the usage of the Dark Arts. Sometimes you have to use it for your own survival, which is fine. But to use it to be vengeful or controlling is the unethical part," Akira said.

"So, Kikaku was meeting in the multi-level garage with some strange guy, huh?"

Akira explained as we continued on our way. "Yeah. I'd never seen him before. He was Japanese, so it wasn't like he was an outsider. He had on street clothes so I couldn't tell if he was a Shimoshuki. He didn't have a kanji on his shirt or anything,"

"Maybe it was just a friend from Mizzaru?" I suggested.

"Could be, but I'm not convinced." Akira stopped not far from Mayumi's house and turned to me. "Kikaku isn't real good at not looking suspicious. Carrying out a mission is one thing, but when you're on your own turf and doing something you know you'll get in trouble for doing, that's where Kikaku gets into trouble."

"How'd you figure that out?"

"Your creepy little buddy, Morgan."

A slight smile touched the corners of my mouth. Morgan. The infiltrator. I was actually getting fond of the little oddball. "Ah, come on now. He's not that creepy," I said.

Akira looked at me with a blank expression, and said, "Yeah, he is."

I chuckled. Interaction with Akira had lightened my heart and I didn't feel as upset as when I'd left home a short while ago. Perhaps I had more friends than I realized? It was a nice feeling to have people watching my back, to actually want to share information that would help me and save me from a bad situation.

"Thanks again for the help back there," I said.

"That's what Shinobi do," he said, then looked at the ground and added, "That's what friends do."

I was touched, but didn't want to get all sappy. I quickly changed the subject.

"So, you learned how to use your elemental energy?"

"Yeah. Pretty cool, huh?" He looked thoughtfully at his kama and released a breath. His arms jerked slightly as white energy erupted, surrounding the short, sickle-shaped blades. "I haven't gotten used to it yet," he laughed. "Every time I direct the energy to the kama it gives me a little shock."

I looked closely at the white flame. "Are those wolves?" I stared at the continual quick movement of small dogs running, jumping and hiding behind each other and started to wonder if he had the same inner animal as Shinji.

"No, they're foxes."

"Cool. Then you're elemental energy is Earth?"

"Actually it's a Spirit energy. That's why it's white."

I pulled my gaze away from the little foxes dancing lightly around the blades and nodded my head in understanding. It seems everyone was learning this useful tactic.

"Who taught you?"

"My dad," he snorted a sad little laugh. "I know what you're thinking. After you and I had our night out you'd think I'd be finished with his stupid little training thing. But he approached me with this new concept and I couldn't wait to learn. I caught on pretty quick, too. So, now he has a new stupid little training thing using this technique. Just last night he started getting rough with me again – so I let him have it."

"Oh, yeah?"

"Yeah." He lowered his kama, released another breath and the white flames died away. "I'm telling you, Duncan, I'm not gonna put up with his treatment any longer. I used his rough-housing last night as an excuse to give him a black eye and bloody lip. But pretty soon he and I are going to have it out."

I looked at him, not sure what to say. It seemed my conversation with Akira on our way up to the old mill had an impact and I was glad he was finally finding the courage to stand up to his dad.

I slapped him on the shoulder and said, "I'm happy for you, man. Stick with it. But I need to rush off and see my girl before it gets too dark and her mom won't let her come out."

"Sure. No problem. See ya around." He used his flash step and took off.

A few minutes later I knocked on Mayumi's door and was greeted by her mother.

"Good evening, Mrs. Tanaka. Is Mayumi home?" I said bowing.

"Oh, hello Duncan. She's over Lilly's house practicing flower arranging and the use of scented poisons."

Flower arranging with poisons? Not only was she a beautiful delicate, creative lady, she was also deadly and cunning. I thanked Mrs. Tanaka and headed off to Lilly's house.

The sun had almost set and evening shadows stretched out over the Chiao Village. Lilly's house wasn't very far from the other side of town. I bypassed the Elder's Mansion and wound through side streets before cutting through front yards. My mind was processing the new information I had learned from Akira. Though I'd meditated on it, learned more, and tried to piece it all together, what was happening in our village, even between the Shimoshuki, the involvement of the German, and the actions of several teens, well, it still didn't make sense. This whole thing was getting crazy, there didn't seem to be a reason why our own young people would turn against their village. I also couldn't believe the allegations against my sister. That hurt most of all.

As I cleared the end of Main Street and turned toward the garage I noticed three shadowy figures walking along a high ridge. It was the same place where I trailed Uncle and the two Black Dragon escorts. These figures headed in the same direction. I wondered if it was Uncle with escorts yet again and felt intrigued. I wanted to see Mayumi, but the urge to follow the figures was pulling me away. I paused. Contemplated. Looked in the direction of Lilly's house, and then at the figures as they ascended the hill and headed toward several small buildings. Mayumi would understand, I mean, she was busy with Lilly anyway and I didn't want to interrupt their girl thing and be in the way. Besides, this could be important and if it really was Uncle, he might just lead me to the place where the secret item of the Chiao was kept.

Using my flash step I quickly caught up. I melted with the shadows and zipped from tree to tree in an effort to cover my approach. I watched the figures closely. They walked a certain distance then stopped, looked around as if confused, and then made their way to the first building. I closed in, taking advantage that they had their backs to me. I was so very close, but kept a measure of security in the shadows of a tree.

"This can't be it," said the one leading the group. He shut the door of the small shed-like building in distaste and turned to the others accompanying him.

"This doesn't make sense," said another, his shadowy outline suggesting long, unkempt hair, a lean body and a katana at his side. "Didn't you get the map from your contact?" He turned to the other guy accompanying them.

"Sure did. He swore it was correct." This one had a deep voice with the shape of a hulking mass.

"Maybe he gave you the wrong one, or he misled you just to get the money," the leader said.

"I told him I'd kill him if he didn't give me the correct coordinates," said the big guy. I suddenly knew who it was - the big Shimoshuki and his two friends.

"Come on, we're wasting time," said Straggly Hair.

I had to stop them, but I couldn't use my inner presence. I was afraid it might take over completely and I would lose control again. Big Guy already had a taste of my power. The other ones had only heard about it from him and possibly saw me in action when I saved Hikaru weeks ago. I was taking a chance, yet had to do something. To capture them on our turf would be huge. As soon as they started moving toward the next building I drew both swords and stepped out of the shadows.

"Stop right there!" I demanded.

The three instantly drew their swords, turned and sank into fighting stances. Unfortunately, as soon as they saw it was me they relaxed and became cocky.

"Well, well, well, look who we have here." Straggly Hair tapped his blade on his shoulder and gestured toward me as if I was amusing.

"Come back for another ass-kicking?" Big Guy sneered.

"Not gonna happen," I assured them, though I wasn't so sure

myself. These three proved to be more than my match, especially as a unit. They were nasty and cunning and worked like a pack of jackals against their prey.

Leader then mumbled to the others, "Wait a minute. This could be better than the other thing."

"What about...?" Straggly Hair started.

"We'll get it later," Leader demanded, elbowing him. "This is more important." A devious smile spread across his mouth as he looked as me. "Execute."

With that one word the three fanned out around me with blinding speed. With weapons drawn, they laughed and sneered while circling me. I centered, gathered my focus, felt for their presence and waited for their attacks.

In a flash they pressed in on me. I was trapped in one spot unable to move. They slashed and jabbed with their swords, obviously hoping to bleed me enough to weaken me. I felt each attack right before it happened and I blocked, ducked, and evaded, using each dragon sword as if they were separate entities. I felt electric; energy pulsed through me without hearing the voice, without calling upon the inner power. Two attacks came in from either side and I instinctively blocked, briefly held the position then back kicked the third attack coming up from behind. Neither if us were gaining an edge on the other and after fifteen minutes of this brutal game the tables were suddenly turned – on me.

All three suddenly threw smoke pellets, instantly shrouding me in a cloud of smoke. I didn't panic; it was no different than the Dark Room where we learn to fight several opponents, or maneuver and steal items, in a pitch-dark room while blind folded. Unfortunately, these guys took it to the extreme. In a whirlwind of motion they ducked in and out of the smoke cloud, landing punches anywhere they could, taking sucker shots and trying to sweep my feet out from under me. I gathered my Ki in my legs and just as I was about to jump straight up and out of their little circle of doom, Leader appeared in front of me from the cloud, grabbed my shirt front and blew a fine white powder in my face.

The action caught me off guard. The first thing that came to mind was that he had poisoned me, yet I knew from hearing past remarks they wanted me alive. Within seconds the powder took effect. My head swam, the earth tilted and I used my swords like a cane to hold myself steady. That idea didn't work so well and within seconds I fell to one knee, yet desperately held onto my swords. My equilibrium was thrown off and I couldn't balance, my muscles wouldn't respond. The cloud of smoke dissipated and once again the three Shimoshuki surrounded me. They stood still, watched me and waited for something to happen.

"Stop fighting it," Straggly Hair took my swords from my limp hands and slid them into their case on my back.

"Take them, it'll make carrying him easier," Leader said.

"No!" Still on my knee, I blindly swung a back fist at Straggly Hair as he went to remove the case from my back. The effort was useless and I lost my balance and fell to the ground. My mouth became dry, my tongue felt huge and it was becoming difficult to swallow or talk. I rolled onto my back. The night sky spun, my ears rang as if I had come from a rock concert and I was no longer in control of my muscles.

"I think you gave him too much," Big Guy said and threw me over his meaty shoulder.

I knew what was going on; I was completely aware, but could do nothing about it. I was paralyzed. It was maddening. I couldn't even think straight! I just hung there, limp like a rag doll.

"Nah, he's a big strong boy. I'm just waiting for him to pass out," Leader laughed.

"Here, allow me," Straggly Hair said.

The last thing I remember was the rabbit punch to my jaw.

17

The Diabolical Mind of Dr. Yen

My head pounded as I slowly came to. Groggily I focused, drifting in and out of consciousness. It was hard staying fully awake. I didn't know what time it was, what day it was, or what was going on around me. I was in a room, bright lights shining down from above, and people talked beyond my line of vision. They sounded so far away.

A blurry figure of a man approached, a little skinny man with thick glasses that made his eyes appear long and huge. He had something in his hand, smiled down at me, and then I felt the pain, such excruciating pain. I opened my mouth to scream, but no sound came out. Yet in the distance I could hear someone screaming. Was this a dream? Was I dead? This must be hell.

The pain took over and I drifted into darkness once again...

I awoke some time later. This time I was a little more coherent than last. It was quiet in the room, the lights were dim and I was alone. My focus was better and the more I looked around the more I realized I was in some sort of a medical room. Metal tables lined the wall across from me. On them were rows of cutting tools of different sizes and styles. A few had blood on the tiny blades. A tall glass cabinet stood to my left, filled with bottles of different colored liquids; some were clear, still others contained thick brown liquid. Large lights, like those in a surgery room, hung above me and that's when I realized I laid flat on my back on a long metal table and was strapped down.

"What the..." My voice was hoarse and my throat raw. It didn't even sound like me anymore. I desperately needed a drink of water.

I looked down at my wrists, tried to wriggle a hand out of the buckled strap, but it was held tight. With my senses finally focused the reality of what was going on became more surreal. The movements of my hand radiated pain up my arm; my eyes grew wide with horror as I noticed wires and tubes were attached to various areas of my arms. I couldn't believe it! Who did this? Are they nuts?

My breath quickened, fear surged through me. I wanted to rip those things out of me and get away from this place as quickly as possible, but how? Even my ankles were strapped at the base of the table. All I had on was my black workout pants and tabi boots. I was weak, so weak.

"Shit! What the hell are they doing to me?" I croaked, just to prove I still had a voice.

I looked around hoping to find something sharp close by to use, but my captor was smart. He knew a ninja could use practically anything for escape or as a weapon and kept the area close to me clear. Not far were my swords, still in their case, propped against the wall. I wanted them.

Voices drifted from down a hall on the other side of a door and through it emerged the same man I saw through blurry vision once before.

"Ahhh, good. You're awake." He walked over to me and

pulled on a pair of medical gloves. "How are we feeling?"

"Like shit! What's your problem? What are you doing to me?" I spat.

He didn't answer. He smiled, turned his back to me and pulled a small metal table close. My eyes never left him as he piddled with something in his hands. When he turned back around he was adjusting a small black box with switches and wires attached.

"You really are quite a specimen," he said impressed. "Most grown men never regain full consciousness with this type of procedure."

"What?" I whispered, too horrified for words.

"Hmmm, yes, most slip into a coma and die," he smiled a kooky yet crazed sort of smile, as if the thought of doing that type of thing to people didn't faze him in the least. "But you, young man, are exceptional. Yes, it seems the scouts were correct when they said you were special."

"What are you talking about?" I groaned, now feeling the full painful effects of his implants in my arms and chest.

"Why your special abilities, of course. One of our scouts has witnessed you in your primal form. Many of our men have seen you fight unlike anything anyone has ever encountered. That's something quite intriguing to me. I want to find out what this primal form is, what sets it off, what makes you tick?"

"You're mistaken. You've got the wrong guy! I'm just a regular kid."

"Oh, I don't think so. You see..."

Just then the three Shimoshuki teens burst through the door and interrupted what may have been very important information this crazy doctor was about to spill.

"Well, aren't you a pretty sight," Leader crooned. The others chuckled. I noticed that they each now wore an earring in the cartilage of their right ear; each in the shape of a skull and cross bones, a symbol for death and poison. They must've graduated from jerks to assholes.

"How's it coming, Doc?" Straggly Hair said and gestured to me.

"All the preparations are complete. It's just a matter of figuring out what drives his primal force. And if I can get it to surface I may be able to extract it out of him, contain it and use it to our benefit." He cackled a maniacal laugh as if this was the best joke ever. His eyes were wild and he stepped in place like an excited child about to get candy.

"We could use it against his own people," Big Guy said, clearly amused.

"Now, you said you fought him when he was in his primal form?" the doctor asked Big Guy.

"Yeah. He's fully mastered his elemental attacks to the point where he could level a forest. His appearance gets all...weird, like, I don't know, I couldn't see real good that night. But it wasn't natural, I can tell you that."

The door burst open again and a tall, large man rushed in, hobbling on a cane with his leg and arm in a splint. "Doctor Yen, have you finished with your experiments on this one yet?"

"No Lord Tatsuya, I'm only halfway done," Doctor Yen held up a crooked finger and flashed the man a large smile.

I focused on the large man and reflected on the name. Tatsuya. That was the name of the Shimoshuki leader from long ago. So, this must be the great-great grandson and now the new leader, the one encouraging his people to attack us for the sake of something that the Chiao have. I wanted to say something to him, but wasn't sure what. He may not listen to me anyway; after all, he was the man I landed on when I jumped from the tree the day I saved Hikaru and all but slaughtered fifty of his men. I must've broken his leg and arm in the process. Better yet, maybe I should just keep my mouth shut.

"Well, finish up. I want you to focus on the new poisons. We have preparations to make and only a month to finish. You've had him for two days now. Finish up!" He turned on his heel and rushed out of the room in a fit of annoyed anger.

Two days? I've been here for two days! Uncle had to be crazy with worry about me, and my friends and sensei, too. Surely they were out looking for me. Then again, Uncle did say that there were times when a Shinobi would be sacrificed. Maybe this was one of those times? I did make a promise to him, saying that when my time came I would face it bravely. I sighed knowing I would have to get free on my own, or die.

"Okay, you three shoo," Doctor Yen ushered my rivals out of the room. When we were alone he approached me while handling the small black box and loomed over me.

My heart pounded out of control and a rush of fear flooded my very soul.

"Okay, now where were we?"

"Water," I whispered. "Please. I need water."

I hoped to confuse him and force a delay. Without protest, he reached for a bottle of water close by and sloppily poured some into my mouth. I drank greedily, not worrying about what ran down the sides of my face. This distraction worked and I wondered how many other things I could think of to make him lose time experimenting on me.

Once done, Doctor Yen flipped a switch that raised the top of the table to a slight inclined position. I was a bit annoyed that he didn't think to do that first before giving me the water.

He then touched a yellow wire attached to my chest, pinched it, and let out a little chuckle when I shrieked as my body jerked uncontrollably. He did the same to the green and red wires on my arms.

"Stop! Please stop! What are you doing?" I shouted, panting in pain.

"Just making sure everything is working. This box is attached to everything you see on your body. With the right combination of impulses I'm sure I can get your primal force to rise to the surface."

Suddenly the door opened and closed. When we looked, no one was there. Then the jars in the glass cabinet clinked together as if moved from some unseen force. When the doctor looked, no one was there.

"Are you sure you know what you're doing?"

Suddenly shaking like a rabbit, Doctor Yen looked across to the other side of the room where the voice came from. I looked as well. There, lingering in the only shadows of the room was a tall man, thickly built and concealed in tight-fitting black ninja attire. He wore knee-high leather tabi boots with at least five kuni tucked up the outside of each boot, as well as a leather belt with small pouches and custom-made weapons unlike anything I had ever seen. His arms were bare save for the bracers that covered his forearms; these were each armed with a row of small steel blades. He wore a hood adorned with a metal headband, carved with an intricate design of a crane and tiger swirled in battle. A facemask covered all but his elderly eyes. He casually leaned against the wall, arms crossed over his broad chest and ankles crossed, looking like he was here for a friendly visit.

"You gonna speak, old man?" His voice was deep and cold as steel. His eyes held no emotion, but his mannerism gave the impression he expected an answer soon.

"Y-yes, yes, Master Tsubasa. I do know what I'm doing, I assure you," Doctor Yen squeaked out, his hands shaking as he adjusted the box in his grip.

I sucked in my breath at the mention of his name. So, this is the guy Morgan mentioned the other day, the legendary assassin from the Tesenga Clan. He was the one the Shimoshuki sought out for his services. For some reason he looked familiar. I scanned his appearance once again and lingered on the bracers. Hmm, I'd seen them before. The row of blades ran in a single line along the outside of each bracer. They even looked like they could stand up to slice...wait a minute...that night in the forest... the Shadow Master!

"Here he is. You can kill him now if you'd like." Doctor Yen gestured to me.

What did he say? That sounded like an invitation to kill his target. Me?

Master Tsubasa walked over to me, glanced down at my pathetic form and snorted lightly as he passed. "Not a challenge like that. I don't do mercy killings."

In a blink of an eye he was gone. The door barely moved as it silently closed behind him.

So it was true then. I really was his target. He could've killed me that night in the forest, but he didn't. Maybe he was testing me, feeling me out to see what kind of a challenge I would be.

With the dark assassin gone, Doctor Yen quickly went to work on me, flipping switches, touching wires, trying all sorts of combinations to force my inner entity to surface. I shrieked and cursed and vomited over and over for what seemed like hours. My head hurt, my body screamed with pain, I wanted to summon my Ki but didn't have the strength. It seemed the time for the doctor to stop experimenting and leave me alone would never come.

He finally paused and walked over to the table lined with cutting tools. My eyes widened as I watched him pick each one up and measure the tiny blades; some dirty, some rusty and some with dried blood caked on. Panic now set in. I had to get out of here! I had to get loose! I needed help - please, inner voice where were you?

I had to find that voice. I buried it deep last time it surfaced when I attacked Shinji. I tucked it away in a place away from my Ki, yet it was part of my Ki, seemingly attached. Where was it? I couldn't relax and breathe. I couldn't concentrate and focus. My mind was a whirlwind of panic and fear, anger and despair, and the last thing I could do was focus on where I put the inner personality.

Wait a minute - anger. That's it. My anger...

I fed my fear to my inner anger, drew it deep inside and allowed myself to become livid over what was happening to me. My emotions flew out of control as I concentrated on the pain, the discomfort and the dislike for this tiny old man inflicting it upon me. The desire for death consumed me and conquest was at the front of my mind. I allowed it all to take over, to occupy my very soul.

Warmth radiated from my center, quickly spread throughout my body and lent me renewed energy and strength. I welcomed it. Something pulsed beneath my skin, tickled the back of my mind, and I knew then what it was.

What has happened to the vessel!

The It was back and not happy with what had happened to me.

18

Fallen

Doctor Yen hummed a little tune to himself as he chose a knife for his next experiment. He paused briefly at the sound of my movement on the metal table and the clinking of buckles. My eyes bored into his back as I watched him closely. He stopped to listen to what was going on behind him, only to shrug it off. Obviously he felt I was struggling while his back was turned, but was too confident that I couldn't get away. It wasn't until he turned around that he learned how wrong he was.

His expression changed from surprise to horror as he came face to face with the very thing he was trying to draw from my body. I balanced on the little footrest at the bottom of the tilted table, giving the impression I was much taller. We held each other's gaze as he looked into my eyes now black as stones. He noticed what I could feel: my veins protruded and pulsed with life all over my arms, neck and upper body, my hair swirled gently as if on a breeze. He staggered back once he looked down and saw that the thick leather straps that had held my limbs in place were now snapped in half. His eyes widened as he witnessed, one-by-one, the wires and tubes in my arms and chest drop from my body, the insertion points closed up and healed.

I stepped down from the table and slowly advanced. The power within overwhelmed me and it was all I could do to maintain a measure of control, but it was winning. I felt my appearance darken and my hair stirred around my face like it was alive with electricity. Dr. Yen moved his mouth but no words came out. *Pish!* No matter. Pathetic human. It was all for the best anyway.

Gathering more power, I took one long step and covered the gap between us in an instant, snatched him up by his throat and squeezed. He gagged for air, his feet left the floor and his legs shuddered as I brought him close to my face and looked into his eyes - the window to the soul. In that moment I saw a lifetime of senseless deaths and experiments, suffering and pain that this human had committed against man and beast. I loathed his very presence...he needed to die.

Without a care I crushed his windpipe and ripped it from his throat. His corpse flopped to the floor and blood pooled around his head, now barely attached to his body. I gazed at the windpipe in my hand. Such a simple device, yet necessary for life. And the blood - so much blood - the giver of life. I contemplated this thought as I studied the doctor's windpipe in my hand, dropped it to the floor, and then moved my fingers around slowly, admiring how the blood shone on my skin.

Voices echoed down the hall from the other side of the door and snapped me back to the present. I dismissed the thoughts of life and death, for they were not my own, even though I shared the same thoughts and visions with the inner voice taking over my body. This time the takeover seemed gentler, almost kind, as if the thing inside was nurturing me and testing how much further it could go within the confines of my body. I allowed it in my head and shared its thoughts on life and death, but now wanted to be in control of my own physical choices and I let it know with one firm command.

Thanks, but this is my body and I'll take it from here.

The thing didn't protest, but stayed with me. Power and magic crackled on the surface as I continued to move of my own accord. I grabbed my sword case, strapped it to my bare back and assessed any escape routes from the medical room, while wiping the doctor's blood from my hand. I had to move fast, the voices were very close now.

There were no windows, only one door, but there was the novelty of a drop ceiling. I ran at the corner of a wall, bounded from each side stepping to the right, then left, then popped one square ceiling tile open while jumping through. I quietly landed with my feet on either side of the metal supports and carefully put the ceiling tile back in place, just as several people entered the room. They stopped short, gasped, and a round of comments followed.

"What the hell!" someone shouted.

"Dr. Yen!" shouted another.

"Who did this?" a third person commented.

"It could only be one person!"

"How'd he get away?"

"I don't care, just find him!"

The scuffle of tabi boots signaled that the search was on and I heard them burst out of the room, leaving the doctor's body to lie as I'd left it. Keeping in mind that one person may have stayed behind in the room to see if I'd come out of hiding, I stilled my breath and kept my movement light as a cat as I scanned the upper ceiling for a way out.

The area was dark, save for a few slivers of light coming through tiny air vents in the roof. The space was low and cramped and I had to move like a spider across the drop ceiling, stepping only on the few support beams and connectors or I'd fall through and wind up back in the medical room. Moving as quietly as I could I cleared the medical room ceiling and found a connecting space. The space was small, only two feet by two feet, but I was able to maneuver through it. Once done, more drop ceiling tiles lay before me. I silently removed a tile and looked down. A long hallway was below me. Closed doors lined either side and no people were in sight. I replaced the tile and slowly made my way to the other side of the drop ceiling, removed a tile and looked down. It was the same hallway, just the other side. Suddenly a door burst open. Several overly excited Shimoshuki emerged. I gently replaced the tile, but left just enough room so I could watch them and listen in on their conversation.

"Okay, men. That kid from the Chiao broke free and killed the doctor. For all we know he's on a killing spree..." came the voice of a man that sounded in charge.

"How do we know he's still in the village?" a subordinate asked. The other men mumbled an agreement to the question.

"We don't. The entire perimeter of the village has been locked down. No one gets in or out until he's found. Use whatever force is necessary to capture him."

"Alive?"

"Of course." Their boss shot back.

"But Doc is dead. What else could we need him for?"

"I say we kill him on sight!"

"You'll follow orders! Got me?" The boss barked loudly. His men fell silent. "Lord Tatsuya has plans of his own. Now get out there and find him!"

The small crowd of men scattered. The hallway fell silent once more.

I rested in a squat position, ran a hand through my long hair as it continuously lifted and moved from the power of my inner presence, and then blew out a troubled breath.

"This doesn't look good," I thought to myself, and the voice, if it was listening.

We can take 'em, you know...

"That doesn't sound like you at all," I whispered, more to myself yet understood the It heard my every sound and thought. Then I wondered if It was trying to relate to me.

We could be as one...

"Yeah, we could," I snorted at my disinterested comment and shook my head.

You need me to survive...

"Well, that's true, but not all the time," I reasoned.

Conquer all...

I balked. This comment was against all that a true ninja believed. We were taught to preserve life; kill only when necessary. When it was our job, when we had a contract, and when we had to defend our lives, only then was it necessary. It was clear to me that this voice was not a part of my ninja heritage. It was something different, alien to me, something that used me for its purpose and I had to learn to live with it – somehow. For now this conversation with the It was over and just when I decided to block the It out of my mind the power radiating off of me disappeared, yet I could still barely feel the inner presence in my gut. I returned to my normal self and weakness took over, hunger and thirst raged and I felt lightheaded. I wasn't sure what just happened and summed it up to the thing inside me getting angry. Whatever the issue, I decided now was the time to move.

Once all was quiet in the hallway I dropped down, rounded a corner and headed through several doors. The smell of food wafted down a corridor and my stomach growled in protest. I hadn't had anything to eat in two days. I needed to grab a bite to eat, even a small bowl of rice, just to get me through.

I found the swinging doors that led to the kitchen and pushed one open just a crack. Inside was bustling with action, just like at The Jade Tree. Cooks were calling back and forth, knives chopping and at least a dozen pans and woks were steaming and sizzling all at the same time. My keen ninja eyes scanned the kitchen and spied an entire tray of rice balls sitting very close to the door. My stomach knotted with hunger; I had to have just one.

With all the activity going on, I was hoping to slip in unseen, snatch a rice ball and slip out. All was going according to plan as I sunk low in a crouch, snuck in and hid next to the table. No one noticed. This was perfect. Keeping a wary eye on the cooks, I reached up and took a rice ball, stuffing as much of it in my mouth as possible before I could even back away. The more I chewed, the more I wanted and the messier the floor around me became. I was so crazed with eating I didn't even notice – it was sloppy and amateurish of me and even as I made it out into the hallway I didn't think to check for the trail of rice dropping from my hands and pants as I finished the rice ball and walked away.

A shout rang out and at least twelve cooks burst from the kitchen, following the rice trail. That's when I ran.

I bolted down the hall and burst through the first door I came to. I knew it wasn't the best course of action for a top Shinobi, but in my present state I felt evading and escaping was the best thing to do. I may have been coursing with power from my inner presence on the inside, but outside my body was in pain, I was exhausted, weak from hunger and thirst and my Ki was running out. I couldn't keep a healthy balance of Ki between myself and the inner presence. It was taking from me, as well as giving, sitting on the edge of my Ki, seemingly waiting for me to relinquish complete control and let it do as it will. After the attack on Shinji

I was terrified to let that happen again. This time I may not be able to come back...

I entered a vast room, large enough for meetings, gatherings or ceremonies. Chairs and tables were pushed to the sides and a stage was at the far end and windows lined the walls. I glanced outside. It was late afternoon and I desperately wanted to get home. There were also four exit doors at each corner and I headed toward the nearest one.

Four Shimoshuki emerged through the door with swords, chain whips and kuni drawn. Four more entered at the far end bearing similar weapons. I drew both dragon swords and slowly backed up toward a row of windows, yet kept my adversary in sight. The eight Shimoshuki closed in and spread out around me, boxing me in. They swung their chain whips in anticipation, flipped kuni around their fingers, and readied their katana. My training instantly kicked in. I focused on all of them at once, settled within myself, felt their presence and prepared for the first move. The It was ready too, and it seethed and whined in my head.

Destroy them all...

No! I said in my head. *This will not be a bloodbath.*

The vessel is weak and sick. It weakens me to sustain it...

Things started to make sense. The presence could only heal me and keep me going up to a certain point. Time was running out. The ninja were closing in, getting anxious for a kill.

I'm using up my Ki? I thought.

Yes...life force...

My vision was suddenly a little fuzzy, I staggered slightly and the men surrounding me noticed. They cast each other amused grins. I was in trouble.

How can we keep going before I collapse?

Give me all of you...

Now the reasoning clicked. The only way I was going to survive this was if I let this thing take me over completely. That meant I'd wind up slaughtering the entire village, because deep inside that's what I wanted to do...and the It knew. It knew my darkest thoughts. Consciously I would never do such a thing, but if I let this presence take over I would never know what I was doing. I would drift into the Darkness like before when I attacked Shinji. I was barely able to come back to myself that time. What would happen this time? The thought terrified me and the presence fed off of my fear, gobbling up more Ki. I swooned and planted my feet firmly, held my swords in a guard position and tried not to let my attackers know that I was ready to pass out. My arms felts weak, my legs trembled slightly and my muscles weren't responding very well. I was almost out of Ki and the inner presence couldn't keep sustaining me unless I gave myself over.

A whip cracked and sliced my shoulder, jerking all of my senses to high alert. I responded by attacking the first ninja that tried to get behind me with a double blade slice, catching his chain whip and ripping it from his hands then slicing his cheek. I then followed through with a powerful front snap kick, knocking him backwards so hard he took three men down with him. The others moved in quickly. In a whirlwind of motion my attackers came at me with all they had; slashing, punching, kicking, spinning, and trying their best to damage and weaken me. With only the help of a thin layer of power left from my inner presence I defended and attacked. Keeping close to the windows and not allowing anyone to get behind me, I blocked, kicked and took control of the fight.

I faltered. My focus faded, too many kuni got through my defenses and stuck me in various places as a katana sliced my forearm and the men closed in. I chanced a glance over my shoulder at the windows and that's when a katana found home – the blade burned as it pierced my side. I looked down, saw the blood and went insane.

Using my last bit of Ki I side-kicked the man, dislodging the blade, and threw him into his brothers. In a sweeping motion with my blades, I met the other Shimoshuki weapons head on, swept them off to the side, channeled my ninpo and did a round-house kick that sent them toppling like dominos.

They were all on the floor, tangled and scrabbling for their weapons. With minimal damage and no deaths, I felt satisfied that I had done what was expected of me as a Shinobi of the Chiao. I turned, ran and smashed through a window. Shards of glass stuck out of my shoulders, arms and chest as I blindly ran through the village.

Shouts rang out as Shimoshuki ninja spotted me. The pounding of feet followed far behind. I pushed for more power, the inner voice protesting as I went, but I wouldn't give in to its demands. I had to get away. I had to heal, to regain my own personal strength.

The tables had drastically turned on me. I was now hunted, wounded, bleeding, exhausted and ready to pass out. I was pushed to the brink of wanting to give up just so I could sleep and regain my strength. But I couldn't. To do so would mean being strapped down on another table, or left in a dark cell with no food, water or warmth, possibly to be tormented and tortured. Uncle would never know what happened to me. No! I had to keep going. I wouldn't give up – ever! I made that promise to Uncle long ago.

The forest greeted me as I grabbed onto a thin pine and panted, blood flowed down my body. The crowd that hunted me had grown in numbers. Somehow I had to escape.

19

Hand of Fate

I landed in a shallow part of the river with a bone-jarring splash. Exhausted and filthy, I laid in the cool water, allowing the current to wash over me, soothe my wounds and cleanse the vomit, blood and waste off my body and pants. Blood from where the katana ran me through trickled into the water and washed down stream. I was so very weak and I just wanted to lie in the water and die.

The inner voice was silent now, its power faded. But without the power I could now feel every inch of pain, every wound from kuni attacks, every slice from the glass still sticking out of my body and the katana wound in my side burned like fire. This was more than any young man not quite seventeen should endure. But I was an assassin, trained in the way of the ninja - a world apart from other kids.

Shouts echoed throughout the forest. I had to get up. Get moving. Don't stop. That's what the enemy would want me to do, just give up, and succumb to death.

"'What if you were in enemy territory and being hunted?'"

Master Katsumi's voice echoed in my head.

Things he harped on came to mind and all he repeated day after day suddenly made sense. So, this is what he meant. This is what it felt like to be on the brink of death, alone, and hunted. Now I could feel that his words rang true and it made me wonder if he must've experienced something similar.

"'If you can keep calm even in the face of danger, you can think things through,'" was the wise voice of Yamamoto sensei. He always knew the right thing to say at the right time. He was right, however. I couldn't panic – not yet.

I shivered. Footsteps drew near. I rose from the water, stayed in a crouched position and surveyed the land, while picking glass out of my arms and chest. Dozens of Shimoshuki searched for me among the trees. Escape was cut off on two sides. The only way to go was downstream, which would lead me toward the Chiao village, but not close enough. They would still have the advantage of cutting me down before I even made it to our borders. The other way was up the mountain toward the top of the waterfall. This way allowed for more cover and a better chance of circling around, losing my pursuers and making it back home the long way around. The downfall was that I had more time to bleed to death.

I scooped water up in my hands to drink and mulled the decision over in my mind. I didn't have a whole lot of time to bat this around. Determination set in as I made my choice. Keeping low to the ground I stepped out of the stream and continued through the forest, ducked from tree to tree and headed up the mountain.

I moved as quietly as I could through the forest, using the slightest magic I could muster and taking care to not leave footprints in the earth. My pursuers weren't easily fooled, however. The pace they kept was mind-blowing, no matter how I covered my tracks and tried not to break any sticks or branches. There was only one way they were able to stay on my trail - blood. This was one thing I couldn't stop and I had no rags to blot or tie off the flow; I could only press the area with my right hand. I was weak from a lack of nourishment and loss of blood, but I kept going. With determined strides I forced myself to trudge up the mountain. The terrain turned from a dense forest to sparse trees and large croppings of rocks, boulders and brush. My cover was almost lost and I had to use nature to the best of my ability. The roar of the waterfall was close and helped mask my footfalls. It added a small touch of comfort as well.

Twilight was almost upon the mountain, a time when shadows played tricks with your mind. Being in no physical condition to fight, I found myself jumping at every sound, at the slightest movement of branches, and at the shadows that played on the ground. The Shimoshuki had proven to be ruthless and cunning. I wouldn't be surprised if they weren't already ahead of me just waiting for me to walk into a trap. But the shadows...they seemed to move on their own, as if someone had breathed life into them.

I paused and scanned the area with my eyes. Off to my left a shadow seemed to shrink back from my gaze. Then suddenly to my right a long shadow thrown off by a tree bent and moved unnaturally. What was going on? Were all the Shimoshuki ninja endowed with this unique ability? This was highly unusual of course, for only someone born with this special ability, handed down through the generations, could achieve such stealth and deceit.

Then I remembered...the Shadow Master...

Master Tsubasa. Only a matter of days ago I was his target - a price put on my head by the three Shimoshuki teens. He pursued me that one night, had the opportunity, but didn't kill me. Doctor Yen offered my life to him earlier today, but he wasn't the least bit interested. I wasn't a challenge, strapped down and pathetic. So, what was I now?

Several things - I changed into my inner demon form. I killed. I evaded and got away in my weakest state. Perhaps now I was a worthy opponent and he was out here, somewhere, waiting for me. I didn't want to think about it.

I took off at a slow trot, keeping a wary eye on my surroundings and listening for the sounds of approaching footsteps. Night creatures were awake and the forest was alive with their sounds and movements. The closer I got to the waterfall, the more it drowned out the surrounding sounds, but it didn't take away from the metallic ring of six katana being unsheathed.

In the moment that it took for me to spin around to face them I was surrounded by Shimoshuki ninja. They spread out before me, wary yet steadily closing in. I drew one dragon sword from the sheath on my back, my other hand pressed on my bleeding wound. I panted as blood seeped through my fingers and dripped to the ground. I planted my feet firmly and held my ground even though it was quite clear I was in pain and exhausted. I scanned the area for an escape before it got too dark. Off to my right and slightly behind me was the old mill. The looming structure looked ominous against the rocks and darkening sky, and the creaking of the water wheel was barely heard from so far away. It gave me an idea.

I turned and ran toward the old mill, zigzagging around trees and rocks, engaging the enemy in swordplay and forcing them to strike nature more so than me. I used the terrain to my advantage, popping out around trees, as a katana, aimed for my head, struck the tree instead. Gouges and slashes marked nature, feet pounded around noisily, smashing down the earth. Our fighting was so loud the night creatures fell silent and went into hiding. I steadily backed up toward the old mill with the enemy pressing in. I was very close to my destination, but with no possibility of escape. Ninja were bearing down on me from all sides, the old mill at my back, darkness had completely fallen and there didn't seem any chance of a rescue.

Until...

A groan echoed, low and deep, bouncing off rocks and trees, and then ended in a gurgling sound that I had heard only once before. Everyone stopped to listen. It was followed by several other groans that seemed to speak to each other. The ground trembled slightly as a mountain troll emerged from a nearby boulder, pulling away from, yet seemingly a part of, the giant chunk of stone.

Another troll rose from the ground and yet another material-ized from the trees. The Shimoshuki froze in their tracks, not sure what to do, but I remembered all too well the actions and fighting skills of the trolls. The giant creatures paused and looked from side to side, sniffing the air and becoming agitated. Their tiny eyes flashed in the night.

With the mountain trolls now standing between me and the Shimoshuki, I used the opportunity to duck close to a wall of the old mill. I squatted down behind a cropping of thorny bushes and scooped up a handful of soft wet earth. Gritting my teeth I pressed it to my wound to hide the smell of blood and hopefully stop the bleeding. I wanted them to target my enemy and not me.

"Don't just stand there, men, attack!" shouted one of the Shi-moshuki.

The ninja hesitated at first, but when a troll came lumbering their way, swinging its spiked club, they kicked into action. Swords clanged against clubs, spikes pierced skin and men shrieked. The trolls plodded and stomped around, trying to smash the ninja into the earth any way possible. It was payback for damaging the forest.

The Shimoshuki ran circles around the trolls, throwing stars and spikes at their legs in an attempt to slow them down. It worked for Akira and me, but not this time. As I watched the scene unfold from my place of safety, I deduced that the trolls remembered and learned after their confrontation with us. The ungainly beasts managed to fend off all attacks, pulled stars, spikes and kuni out of their hairy bodies, and threw them back at the ninja.

After all attempts failed at chasing off the trolls, the tables were turned and the trolls managed to chase off the Shimoshuki. The men finally gave up trying to capture me and fled down the dark mountain with the trolls close on their heels. Their shouts of alarm and warning echoed from the forest until they were no longer audible. I sat as still as possible, quieting my labored breathing, until I could no longer hear them and the night creatures resumed their activities and songs. After a short while I decided it was time to go.

At first I couldn't move. My legs didn't want to respond and I staggered slightly in my attempt to stand. I swooned and leaned heavily against the wall of the old mill, and then retched. I staggered over to the edge of the waterfall, gaining purchase on the slippery rocks until I spied a shallow pool of water among them. I fell to my knees, shoved my face into the cool water and washed vomit, blood and dirt from my hands and face. Tiny fish residing in the pool darted around to gobble up the leftovers and I sat heavily on the ground to watch them.

I was lightheaded and nauseous. I needed something to eat and I had lost too much blood. The rice ball from earlier today wasn't enough and the fish weren't even a morsel. This was more than any kid not quiet seventeen should endure. But I was a ninja, highly trained in survival off the land, and then I stopped and snorted at myself for thinking so arrogantly.

"How many Chiao ninja had this kind of crap happen to them?" I mused to myself.

I knew from stories Uncle told that my father underwent a similar situation, as well as several of his men. Most didn't survive, but my father made it back with one man. His name remained a mystery. I looked up at the clear night sky.

"I won't let you down, father," I said to a star I picked out from the many.

I may have been arrogant about my training, but much of it was true. The Chiao trained the best assassins in the world, and we were sought out from every nation. The Black Dragon Squad was the best, and I wasn't about to forget my future place among them.

Determination set in as I got my head together, forced myself to stand up and gingerly picked my way across the slippery rocks at the top of the waterfall. I maneuver my way across the wide expanse and looked down at the black, churning water that plunged into a fifty-foot drop and thought of the great dragon of the waterfall, the tengu and my red Dragon Stone. I silently said a thank you that it was safe at home with Uncle – forgotten in my pouch, in my room, after I left home to go visit Mayumi. That was two days ago and now with nightfall it will soon be day three.

I had to get home. Captain Yoshida and the elders would want to know what the Shimoshuki have been up to – experiments, poisons and anything else I could remember.

I lept from a boulder to the ground, favoring my side and checking that the mudpack held. It had dried and cracked slightly, allowing blood to ooze. The dark forest now teemed with life and the clouds that drifted in the night sky covered, exposed and uncovered the bright stars, allowing dim light to illuminate my way for a fleeting moment here and there. Without the moonlight most people would find it hard to navigate the woods, but not me. I knew this forest well, especially the area close to the waterfall. And I also knew that I only had about two miles to go to get home. I breathed a sigh of relief, let my guard down and started to trudge home.

That was my first mistake.

I hadn't gone very far when I caught the movement of the shadows as I passed trees and rock. From all different areas behind me, shadows of various shapes and sized ran like liquid along the ground and pooled beneath a very large tree close to me and off to my left. It was a very special Inton Jutsu of Concealment and Camouflage. Fear gripped my heart as I watched in horror the shadows rise up and take on the form of a man. He was dressed all in tight fitting black, his tall, thick build much like Master Katsumi's and his arms were bare save for the bracers that covered the forearms. He wore a black ninja mask and hood and only his elderly eyes were exposed.

I knew this man and caught my breath when I noticed his hand and arm move so fast it was a blur. The metallic *zing!* of a kuni resounded as it struck the tree next to me, sticking out only an inch away from my head. It snapped me back to reality and I ran...

20

Shadow Prophecy

The Shadow Master wasted no time in his pursuit and I knew running wasn't going to be an option. I would have to use my own version of Inton Jutsu, but I needed to get well ahead of him. That wasn't going to be easy. He was hot on my trail. Though I used the forest for cover, stars and spikes barely missed me as I zipped through the trees. I grabbed a few when I could without slowing down. Melting with the night, I feigned left when I actually went right, then soundlessly stepped into the shadows of an old tree and seemingly disappeared. My pursuer went right past me.

"Stop running, boy!" he shouted. Though his voice sounded like he was far away, I had a feeling he was actually only several feet away. Perhaps he was hiding close by, projecting his voice using the Black Arts in the hopes I would fall for his trick and move out of hiding.

Overhead branches jiggled slightly. I followed the movement with my eyes.

"Come out and fight me. I've seen what you can do," he challenged.

I molded my back to the large pine, pressing myself as close as I could and hid in the crooked gap at the base. My heart raced wildly in my chest and my head reeled. What was I to do? Master Tsubasa was expecting me to come out in my full transformed state and give him the ultimate fight. Obviously it would be a fight to the death.

"'Death is not an option,'" Master Katsumi always said, "'It's a coward's way out.'"

But had that coward been held against his will for two days without food or water, tortured, tormented, hunted, stabbed and bleeding to death, would he still be considered a coward for succumbing to death? I contemplated this thought as I continued to listen to Master Tsubasa scouting the area. He knew I was close by.

Please voice, you have to help me, I silently pleaded.

No response.

If I die, so do you.

Still, no response.

I knew what the It was waiting for and now that I was in even deeper shit I was actually considering the proposition. I wasn't sure what I was more afraid of – death or permanent possession. Maybe they were one and the same?

Silently I unsnapped my swords and pulled one from the sheath on my back. I held the blade in an ice pick grip so no light would glint off of it. I knew that once I moved out of hiding he would zero in on me and battle with no mercy. I would only be able to defend. Unless...

An idea came to mind and I checked my wound to see if the mudpack still held. Yes, but blood seeped through slightly. I would have only one chance at this and would have to get as close to home as possible with little time to spare.

I released a nervous breath, concealed a star in my right hand and held it over my wound, then limped out of hiding. I wanted to project the image of being vulnerable. Just as I suspected, within seconds of my appearance the Shadow Master emerged from the darkness only inches away and reached out his iron grip to take hold of me. I slipped from his grasp, expanded the space between us and turned to face him, sword ready, holding my wound and overly exaggerating how much pain I was in.

"Back off! I'm not who you think I am," I said loudly in a challenging tone. I wouldn't have much time to sway his decision on killing me.

Master Tsubasa stopped just on the edges of the shadows and wrapped them around his body like a cloak. He looked at me. His hard gaze scanned my posture.

"Liar."

"Is this how you want to end your career? As the greatest assassin ever, who killed a kid that was weak, wounded, and bleeding to death?"

"You're more than what you seem." His voice was cold as steel. The shadows fell from his shoulders and dragged behind him as he paced back and forth, never taking his eyes off me. He was like a caged tiger and energy seethed off of him.

"If I was this...whatever...you think I am, then why wouldn't I just kill you right now?" Of course that was a lame reason, but I was grasping at straws, biding time.

"Whatever your reason, I know you're not stupid, kid. Any ninja from the Chiao is a formidable foe." He reached over his head for the large wrapped item on his back, the wrappings fell to the ground as if on cue. "Had you finished your training you would've made an excellent Black Dragon." What the fallen wrappings revealed was a scythe. The staff was wide, in a deep wine color with a gold crane painted down the length. Taking up a fourth of the top was a long, slender half-moon shaped blade.

"It's a shame it's all going to end here." He readied himself in attack position.

Time was up. I had to go now!

I threw the star as a distraction, but to my amazement he simply gestured with his hand and raised a veil of darkness. The star disappeared into it. It didn't make the sound of sticking into a tree. It didn't thud on the ground. It didn't make any sound at all. I whipped out my other dragon sword and backed away. With a few simple slashes I took down several young pines at their base. They fell on the Shadow Master with a *thud* and it was enough of a diversion for me to run.

I zipped through the dark forest as if it were daylight, seeking out the deepest shadows and hugging the trees for cover. Master Tsubasa wasn't far behind. And though I couldn't hear him, I could *feel* him. His very presence within the shadows raised unease and even the night creatures quieted and shrank back as he passed.

Out of the deepest shadows a bola whizzed toward me, wrapped around my knees and threw me to the ground. I landed on my stomach, tearing open my wound, the pain was like wild fire in my gut and I cried out. Using my sword I cut the taut leather around my legs, gathered the little bit of Ki I had left and tried to run once more. Master Tsubasa leaped down from a tree, landing in front of me, the blades on his bracers raised, ready to slice, and the scythe hacked at my chest. I skidded to a halt and slashed with my swords, forgetting all protocols of Kenjutsu and just applying my own techniques. Overhead strike, slashing from side to side, and even spinning strikes, it didn't matter, he blocked them all. It was like he was toying with me, waiting for me to get tired so he could finish me off. Problem was, I don't think I was even close to the fighting level he anticipated. I was draining fast. My focus was thrown off, my movements were sluggish.

A powerful backhand caught me across the face and slammed me into the nearest tree. I slid to my knees as pain vibrated throughout my body. My cheek and shoulder were cut open by his bracer blades, but I didn't have time to worry about that now. Only seconds ticked by until I was grabbed by the shoulders, lifted and turned around to face him. I used that opportunity to grab one of his own kuni from his boot as he forced me to stand and stabbed him in the side. I pushed and twisted the knife as deep as I could until he finally cried out in pain. He punched me in the face so hard I flew backwards and landed on the ground. I used that opportunity to scramble to my feet and run like hell. However, I didn't get far.

The shadows rose up before me, taking the shape of the Shadow Master. I feebly backed away and was met by another backhand.

"Where is it, boy?" he shouted, holding the scythe but not using it.

I staggered. Spat blood. Turned to face him. Another backhand. I staggered again.

"Stop toying with me!" he demanded, slowly advancing each time I fell back.

I was fading fast, weak, damaged and practically unable to defend myself any longer.

Voice, please, I beg you

Another backhand and now the shadows around me started to press in, suffocating me. I clung to my swords, trying my best to raise them for defense, but the attacks were coming too fast. The half moon blade glinted in the starlight.

I need you. I need help. I silently pleaded over and over, but the voice ignored me.

The shadows themselves struck me this time and the force spun me around. I dropped to the ground on my hands and knees, face bruised and swollen, lip split open, gasping for breath all while hoping he'd stop long enough for me to get up. That's when I felt the burning flame of a blade pierce me from back to chest. At first I couldn't move, the shock of what just happened hadn't registered yet, but as I looked down between my shaken and dirty arms I saw the tip of the shiny blade, sticky with blood, protruding from my chest. The Shadow Master had run me through as he stood over me.

Had enough....? The voice cooed faintly in my head.

I actually felt relieved that it was still with me. Darkness tried to take over, I felt myself slipping into a void and then something else - a new life. A spark ignited within me, started warm in my center and spread outward.

Help me... I wondered if it would be enough energy to pull me through?

In time...

Time was not something I had much of.

The Shadow Master put his foot on my back and pulled out his scythe. Blood pooled on the ground between my hands.

"All too easy," he sniffed. "You're pathetic and not worth my time."

My anger flared, my breath quickened, but the pulse of my Ki faded...

Now, now, now I begged.

A breeze picked up around me stirring branches and leaves, the night creatures went silent, and my heart slowed. I flopped to my stomach and just lay there, feeling my life slip away. My foe was still close by. Through slit lids I could see the Shadow Master's boots as he paced back and forth, as if he were waiting for something. I was so very desperate. I wanted to cling to life, but I couldn't feel my heartbeat any longer and my breath was very shallow.

Where's that spark? What happened to my chance?

That's when everything went black...

Also available from Silver Leaf Books:

CLIFFORD B. BOWYER

The Imperium Saga

Fall of the Imperium Trilogy

An evil tyrant weaves a tapestry of deception as he plots to conquer the Imperium. Only a few heroes are brave enough to uncover the mystery and face Zoldex directly. Follow the adventures of the heroes of the realm as they try to preserve the Imperium and confront Zoldex's forces. Their hearts are true and their intentions noble, but will that be enough to overcome such overwhelming odds? Find out in the *Fall of the Imperium Trilogy.*

The Impending Storm, 0974435449, $27.95
The Changing Tides, 0974435457, $27.95
The Siege of Zoldex, 0974435465, $29.95

The Adventures of Kyria

In a time of great darkness, when evil sweeps the land, a prophecy fore-tells the coming of a savior, a child that will defeat the forces of evil and save the world. She is Kyria, the Chosen One.

From the pages of the Imperium Saga, *The Adventures of Kyria* follows the child destined to save the world as she tries to live up to her destiny.

The Child of Prophecy, 0974435406, $5.99
The Awakening, 0974435414, $5.99
The Mage's Council, 0974435422, $5.99
The Shard of Time, 0974435430, $5.99
Trapped in Time, 0974435473, $5.99
Quest for the Shard, 0974435481, $5.99
The Spread of Darkness, 0978778219, $5.99
The Apprentice of Zoldex, 0978778227, $5.99
The Darkness Within, 0978778243, $5.99
The Rescue of Nezbith, 0978778251, $7.99
The Responsibility of Arifos, 1609750217, $7.99
Full Circle, 1609750233, $7.99
and more to come!

ILFANTI

Known as an adventurer, the dwarven Council of Elders member Ilfanti is one of the most famous Mages in the realm. Everyone knows his name, and others flock around his charisma. But even Ilfanti is at a loss for why the Mage's Council is ignoring the fact that Zoldex has returned and none are safe as his plans go unchallenged.

The Empress has been kidnapped while in the midst of trying to unite the races. Her true whereabouts are unknown, but her return is vital to the survival of the Seven Kingdoms. The Mages are doing nothing, and Ilfanti can no longer condone avoiding the obvious signs that are plaguing the realm.

Follow Ilfanti as he returns to a life of an adventurer and battles against time to save the Imperium. Experience the adventure and learn if the charismatic adventurer can complete one last mission in time to save the realm.

Ilfanti and the Orb of Prophecy, 0978778278, $19.95

Tales of the Council of Elders

Tales of the nine Mages who form the Council of Elders, the leading body of the Mage's Council. Some of the most charismatic, influential, and powerful characters in all of the Imperium at last reveal parts of what has led them to be the Masters of all magical beings. Follow the adventures of the Council of Elders from the dawn of Mages straight through to the aftermath of the *Siege of Zoldex*. Written by Imperium Saga creator Clifford B. Bowyer and other Silver Leaf Books authors, including Brandon Barr, Stuart Clark, Mike Lynch, B. Pine, and Brittany Westerberg, and introducing Karen Aragon, Ben Mitchell, and Robb Webb.

Tales of the Council of Elders, 1609750276, $19.95

The Warlord Trilogy

A prequel to the epic fantasy saga introduced by Clifford B. Bowyer in *The Fall of the Imperium Trilogy* chronicles the upbringing and development of the boy who is destined to become a legend. A young Braksis must learn how to survive in a world that threatens to overwhelm him, from the devastating battlefields of the Troll Wars, to the ultimate betrayal of the throne, to finding himself alone and unprotected in a world fraught with peril. Follow the adventures of Braksis as he seeks to survive, forge new alliances, reclaim the Kingdom that is rightfully his, and become the Warlord that he is destined to be.

Falestia, 1609750411, $19.95
Falestian Heir, 1609750438, $19.95
Falestian Legend, 1609750454, $19.95

CLIFFORD B. BOWYER
GEN-OPS

In the not-too-distant future, a catastrophic event decimates much of the surface of the Earth, but also presents an amazing discovery that drew scientists from around the world to work in secrecy of the marvels that it could unlock. Genetic manipulation, enhancement, and augment become the key to evolution, leading to test subjects the surpassed even the most optimistic expectations. Seeing the potential for financial gain, a handful of the scientists betrayed the government by contacting foreign powers and selling the technology to the highest bidders .

The technology is out there, the secret of the GENs is on the open market, and the government agency that had been tasked with recovering the technology or destroying all evidence of its existence has been targeted for assassination. Only one man, former Shadow Recon team leader Logan Stone, can be entrusted to take on this vital mission with any home of containing the situation and erasing all evidence that it ever even happened.

It is a race as Stone and his team fights to keep the true secret of the discovery from coming out and recover that which had been stolen. Gen-Ops combines military, espionage, intrigue, and strong character development in a fast-paced and dangerous not-too-distant future world where the fate of humanity hangs in the balance.

Gen-Ops, 1609750373, $24.95
and more to come!

CLIFFORD B. BOWYER
CONTINUING THE PASSION

Continuing the Passion follows the story of Connor Edmond Blake, a best-selling novelist who, after suffering the tragic and unexpected loss of his father decides that the best way to honor the memory of his father is by carrying on the legacy that his father left behind.

Connor's father, William Edward Blake, a Hall of Fame High School Baseball Coach had led his team to numerous state championships. Most of Connor's memories and moments he shared with his father have something to do with and revolve around the sport of baseball. Connor decides to at least make the attempt to coach a High School team in attempt to honor his father.

Continuing the Passion is seen through the eyes of Connor Blake as he experiences the tragedy of the loss of his father, and his pursuit to help his family find a way to overcome the loss.

Continuing the Passion, 097877826X, $18.95

BEYOND BELIEF

Damon Burke had strong family values, a good career, money, friends, and the foundation for a successful life. But he still wanted more than just success in business, and craved the love of a woman and a family of his own. While he had numerous romances, Damon had always prioritized his career over his personal life and failed to find the elusive one to share it all with. That was until he came across the profile of Cassie Caniglia through an alumni network.

Cassie was gorgeous, exciting, enticing, and rich. With a renewed vigor to find personal happiness, Damon could not help but be allured by her and find himself dreaming of a future together. She was everything he had always been looking for, and more. Accepting that, he knew he had to tread carefully to make sure that his dreams did not wind up rushing and sabotaging reality.

But tragedy began drawing Damon into a most dangerous game where everything and everyone he loved was at risk because of his connection to Cassie. While she fights for her very survival to escape the torment of her mob-connected brother-in-law, Damon finds himself desperately trying to help her even knowing that doing so makes him a target. *Beyond Belief* is a romantic suspense that will lead you down a path so dark and twisted that you will begin to question just what is real and what is mere illusion.

Beyond Belief, 1609750357, $19.95

STUART CLARK

PROJECT
U·L·F

Imprisoned for a crime of passion, Wyatt Dorren is given a second chance at life on the Criminal Rehabilitation Program. Dorren becomes the rarest of breeds: an ex-convict who has become a productive member of society, trapping U.L.F.'s—Unidentified Life Forms—from newly discovered planets and returning with them for exhibition at the Interplanetary Zoo. Dorren inspires loyalty and courage in his team members, but nothing from his dark past, or his years trapping dangerous aliens, can prepare him for what's in store now.

Project U.L.F., 0978778200, $27.95
Project U.L.F.: Reacquisition, 0978778286, $19.95
Project U.L.F.: Outbreak, 1609750470, $19.95

MIKE LYNCH & BRANDON BARR
SKY CHRONICLES

Since the dawn of time, an ancient evil has sought complete and unquestioned dominion over the galaxy, and they have found...us.

The year is 2217 and a fleet of stellar cruisers led by Commander Frank Yamane are about to come face to face with humanity's greatest threat—the Deravan armada. Outnumbered, outclassed, and outgunned, Yamane's plan for stopping them fails; leaving all of humanity at the mercy of an enemy that has shown them none.

Follow the adventures of Commander Frank Yamane and his crew as they struggle to determine whether this will be Earth's finest hour, or the destruction of us all.

Sky Chronicles: When the Sky Fell, 0978778235, $18.95
and more to come!

MIKE LYNCH & BRANDON BARR
AMERICAN MIDNIGHT

Tania Peters had it all—a loving, supportive family, and a future that seemed all but set. But when her mother is killed in a plane crash in the jungles of Ecuador, her world comes crashing down around her. As a result, she adopts a live for today philosophy. Throwing herself into the arms of her boyfriend, Tania seeks all that society says will bring satisfaction and meaning into her life. But she soon realizes this is a lie, and begins to fall under the spell of the Unity Party, a political movement that has swept Robert Allen into the White House. But such allegiances come at a price: complete and unquestioned loyalty to the Party. Despite all the "good" the Party does for society, Tania's devotion to the movement is pushed to the limit when her own father, the Pastor of the Calvary Community Church, is arrested and jailed when he refuses to compromise his religious beliefs. Forced to decide between her past and her future, Tania rediscovers the faith she has long since abandoned, even though such a decision could cost everything she holds dear, including her life.

American Midnight, 1609750195, $19.95

B. PINE
The Draca Wards Saga

In a universe where dragons are supreme sentient beings, it is believed that eight humans will be born with extraordinary supernatural abilities that will give them the power to challenge dragons. Divided into two factions—the Draca Debellos: conquerors of worlds to fuel their powerful magic, and the Draca Tueri: protectors of the worlds and their sentient beings—they tirelessly search for these gifted children to train and bond with to help in their eternal struggle and attempt to end their tenuous deadlock.

Follow the adventures, struggles, and development of these humans who have their innocence shattered at a tender age while trying to learn to live under the influence of powerful beings wishing to use them for their own ends, and growing up in a world of tragedy and horror, betrayal and deception.

Familiar Origins, 1609750314, $19.95
Plights, 1609750497, $19.95
Coming of Age, 1609750519, $19.95
Glimpses of Destiny, 1609750535, $19.95
and more to come!

T.J. PERKINS
SHADOW LEGACY

Growing up ninja in a modern world with ancient customs is difficult, but the Japanese government still has need of them. Training in the Chaio village, home of the best ninja, Duncan Kimura dreams of one day being chosen for the elite special forces–the Black Dragon Squad. But his dreams won't become a reality if he can't control his destructive rage that threatens everyone around him.

Turmoil threatens to tip Duncan's balanced world; rivalries, disputes with other teens, competition, and a beautiful kunoichi–a female ninja. The plague of emotions fuels his anger and an entity hidden deep inside him threatens to surface–it wants out. Follow Duncan through his trials and challenges as he will either lose himself to his rage and become a threat to all he knows and loves, or triumph and become the ninja his people expect of him.

Art of the Ninja - Earth, 160975039X, $19.95
Power of the Ninja - Fire, 1609750551, $15.95
and more to come!

JUSTIN R. SMITH
CONSTANCE FAIRCHILD ADVENTURES

"I was twelve when I realized I was a ghost."

So says Constance Fairchild, an eccentric poetess who is heiress to a fortune—and a girl who, from an early age, has believed that she had been reincarnated.

Orphaned at the age of 14, Constance finds herself in life threatening encounters, a victim of vast conspiracies, and under public scrutiny. With her vast fortune, an unforgettable cast of close confidants, a maturity beyond her years, and a desire to turn around unscrupulous and unethical business practices of her ancestors, Constance desperately tries to find a way to survive her ordeals and experience the adventure that is her life.

The Mills of God, 097443549X, $24.95
The Well of Souls, 0978778294, $19.95

CHRISTOPHER STOOKEY
TERMINAL CARE

Emergency Physician, Phil Pescoe, becomes alarmed by a dramatic increase in deaths on the Alzheimer's Ward. The deaths coincide with the initiation of a new drug study with an experimental and highly promising treatment for the disease to half of the patients on the ward.

Mysteriously, the hospital pushes forward with the study even though six patients have died since the start of the trial. Pescoe teams up with Clara Wong—a brilliant internist with a troubled past—to investigate the situation. Their inquiries lead them unwittingly into the cutthroat world of big-business pharmaceuticals, where they are threatened to be swept up and lost before they have the opportunity to discover the truth behind the elaborate cover-up.

With the death count mounting, Pescoe and Wong race against time to save the patients on the ward and to stop the drug manufacturer from unleashing a dangerous new drug on the general populace.

Terminal Care, 1609750292, $19.95

BRITTANY WESTERBERG
INTO FIRE

The fifteen year old Leora had always planned her entire life around working with her brother and father in their gemsmithing shop. She enjoyed it, she was good at it, and she wanted nothing more than to do it. But fate had other plans for Leora.

On a day like any other, Leora's life was turned upside-down when two strangers visited her and informed her family that she had the power of a Mage—abilities she had always been raised to fear. As they seek to whisk her away and train her in her abilities, Leora must decide whether to remain in the family business, or explore these amazing abilities, and, a potential link to her mother.

Deciding to embrace the adventure, Leora learns that there is a lot more in the world outside her home than she thought. With new allies, challenges, experiences, and problems she never knew even existed, Leora must accept the person she was meant to become or lose everything that ever meant anything to her.

Into Fire, 1609750330, $19.95

And available electronically:

JARED ANGEL
ENDLESS WAR OF THE GODS

In the world of Seibu, an endless war between the gods of Light and Dark threatens to destroy all life. Crevahn, mother of creation, struggles to save her newly created world and all life. Without the help of Vyas, a mighty jiva, and Malla, a humble human, Crevahn will fail. Will Vyas survive and maintain his sanity long enough in his battle against the God of Dark? Will Malla overcome her subordination and inevitable execution in her battle against the God of Light? Find out if the world will end or be saved in this high adventuring tale by debut novelist Jared Angel.

Betraying the God of Light, 1609750616, $9.95
and more to come!

BRIAN BANDELL
mute

Officer Monique "Moni" Williams, has never lived an easy life—with an abusive ex-con father, a two-timing, pistol-wielding ex-boyfriend and a racist boss—it's hard to see how things could possibly get more difficult for her. After she meets a child that she bonds with, Moni must protect the girl from a mysterious threat stalking everyone near the Indian River Lagoon.

A serial killer is on the loose on Florida's Space Coast, and Moni has been put in charge of the key witness in the biggest case of her life: an eight-year-old girl called Mariella. The child has gone mute after losing both her parents one harrowing night. Now, Moni struggles to protect the child and break her silence, while more reports of inexplicable deaths and animals with eerie purple eyes pile up. Her bond with the child is tested by a police force demanding answers. What does the lagoon's rotten stench have to do with a mute little girl? Can Moni save Mariella from what lurks along the water? Who is really facing the most danger? Find out in this suspenseful, page-turner that will keep you guessing until the very end.

Mute, 1609750594, $9.95

CLIFFORD B. BOWYER
SNAPPED

Alex Adams has always had a flair for excitement, the thrill of the moment, and pushing things to the edge. He is, always has been, and knows he always will be, a winner in everything that he does. His competitive nature has always driven him, pushing him to succeed in everything he does. Whether it's the sports he excels in, the academics that come easy to him, the charisma of his social life, or the career that he embraces, Alex only knows how to thrive.

Most who knew him felt he lived the perfect life. Everything came so easily to him, he always seemed so happy, and he even married his high school sweetheart. He had the perfect house, a perfect wife, and a perfect job. Or was it? Alex's world it turned upside-down when a cruel new manager, Maria Thompson, is promoted and becomes his boss. Alex finds himself pushed to the limit, acting in ways and doing things he never thought possible, and beginning to see all aspects of his life unravel all around him. Spiraling out of control, he seeks to find something to cling on to, trying to save his position at work, save his marriage, and save himself as his despair leads him to violence, an affair, and self destructive behavior. Alex knows that, for him, failure is not an option. So, the question becomes... how can one get away with murder?

Snapped is a psychological thriller that challenges even the most sane and successful of individuals and threatens to unleash the darkness locked deep within one's soul when pushed beyond one's limits.

Snapped, 1609750578, $9.95

ROB GULLETTE
THE APOLLO TRILOGY

"We choose to go to the Moon in this decade and do the other things, not because they are easy, but because they are hard...", stated former President Kennedy on September 12, 1962. These words inspired a nation in the initial race to the Moon. Now over half a century later these words are moving the world to action once more.

A terrorist attack on the National Air & Space Museum in Washington, DC ignites a new and more deadly race to the Moon than ever before. Too bad the United States has allowed its manned space program to fall apart. The space shuttles are museum pieces and the International Space Station now belongs to the United Nations.

When intelligence reports reveal China's plan to establish a permanent base on the Moon, former astronaut, U.S. President Olivia Kane is faced with a challenge she must confront: Will nuclear weapons soon be aimed at the United States from above, or will the Moon be the site of the next great war? Find out in this suspense-filled thriller.

Waking Apollo, 1609750608, $9.95
and more to come!

LINDA McCUE
DARK DESTINY

Lisa Melton is a typical college student: she studies at the campus coffee spot, stresses over tests and even goes to parties with her friends. But when she wakes up one morning with no memory of the night before, looking like the victim of an brutal assault, and starts seeing a giant black dog in her dorm room—everything around her starts to spiral wildly out of control. Suddenly, Lisa's life isn't so humdrum anymore as she meets a mysterious and handsome man who seems to know more about her than she seems to even know herself. Who is this man: is he simply a supernatural stalker or is he something more? Lisa has little time to decide what to think of him, before she is tangled up in a web of kidnappings, brutal murders, a pack of strange giant black dogs, and an ancient family feud that takes her overseas and within inches of her own sanity.

Dark Destiny, 1609750586, $9.95

To order any Silver Leaf Books title, check your local bookstore, order through our website at www.SilverLeafBooks.com, or mail a check or money order to:

Silver Leaf Books
P.O. Box 6460, Holliston, MA 01746

Please include $3.95 shipping and handling for the first book and $1.95 each additional book. Massachusetts residents please add 6.25% sales tax. Connecticut residents please add 6.35% sales tax. Payment must accompany all orders.

ABOUT THE AUTHOR

T.J. Perkins is a gifted and well-respected author in the mystery/ suspense genre. A member of the Maryland Writer's Association and Sisters In Crime, her short stories for young readers have appeared in the Ohio State 6th Grade Proficiency Test Preparation Book, *Kid's Highway Magazine,* and Webzine 'New Works Review,' just to name a few. She's placed four times in the CNW/FFWA chapter book competition. Previously self-published, her achievements have been greatly recognized and T.J. is also conducting speaking engagements at colleges and libraries, offering advice to others. Shadow Legacy is her first Silver Leaf Books series.

CPSIA information can be obtained at www.ICGtesting.com
Printed in the USA
BVOW012304240113

311544BV00009B/135/P

9 781609 750558